A STREAK OF LIGHT

A STREAK OF LIGHT

A Lieutenant Shapiro Mystery

by Richard Lockridge

J.B. Lippincott Company
Philadelphia and New York

Printed in the United States of America

For Hildy

A STREAK OF LIGHT

1

Cleo yapped at the bedroom door. Her yapping was peremptory. Humans are sluggards, lie-abeds. She yapped again. Nathan Shapiro said, "All right, dog. We hear you." Cleo didn't believe him. She scratched at the door. Shapiro said, "All *right*," and twisted his long, lean body out of the comfort of his bed. He looked at the watch on his wrist. Ten after seven. On a—yes—relatively bright early-September morning. Not autumn yet, but coming on toward it. Two months ago, Cleo would have yapped her alarm at a little after six.

"I guess it's morning," Rose Shapiro said from her bed. Her voice was muffled with sleep. "Perhaps a cat would have been a better idea."

This was entirely clear to Nathan, or as clear as could be expected at seven ten in the morning. Cats do not have to be walked. On the other hand, their litter boxes have to be changed. Nathan said, "Yes, Doctor," and went into the bathroom. When he came out, Rose was sitting up in bed and stretching. Nathan said, "Good morning, Doctor," to Rose Shapiro, newly Ph.D. And, with her doctorate, newly principal of Clayton High School in Manhattan's Greenwich Village, a sizable subway ride from Brooklyn.

It is Rose's belief, now and then mentioned, that they ought to bus teachers.

Hearing movement and voices, Cleo scratched the door again. She did not yap. It is difficult to yap with the leash in your mouth. But a dog must be ready, even if humans may be laggard.

Shapiro put on enough clothes for the street and, he hoped, for a Friday morning in early September. He did not put on his gun, which was a minor infraction of the rules and regulations of the New York Police Department. He opened the bedroom door, and the little Scottie bounced up against him. He snapped the lead onto her collar, and she guided him to the apartment door. Humans have a limited sense of direction. She thumped down the stairs, and Shapiro thumped after her, with notably less enthusiasm. Unlike Cleo, Nathan is not at his best in the early morning.

The morning sun was slanting on the Brooklyn street. A few people were also slanting on it. There was a slight crispness in the air, and the air could be breathed. It felt a little of fall. The feeling was, of course, illusory. The fresh winds of autumn, which sweep New York City clean, were still weeks away. Last night's thundershower hadn't brought them. It would be October before they roused the city from its muggy summer sloth.

Cleo led Shapiro for several blocks, from curb to curb. Finally she found one to her liking. She yapped approval of herself. Shapiro set the direction this time, and it was toward home. Cleo scampered up the stairs to the second-floor apartment. Surely, by now, even humans would realize it was time for breakfast.

Rose was in the kitchen. Cleo, unleashed, joined her in

an excited rush. "Not under *both* my feet," Rose said. "I'm *getting* it, dog. Nathan?"

Shapiro said, "Yes, Doctor?" The Ph.D. was still new enough to amuse them both a little. Nathan had mentioned the oddity of sleeping with a doctor of philosophy. (In English Literature of the Eighteenth Century.) He had not found the oddity inhibiting.

"They want you to call in," Rose said. "But wait till I bring your coffee."

Nathan did not need to wonder about the "They." He was dialing when Rose came in with coffee. He took the cup and put it down on the telephone stand. He got, "Homicide, Manhattan South, Detective Sanders."

"Shapiro," Nathan said.

"Good morning, sir," Sanders said. "The captain called in. Said to call you. There's been a killing at the *Sentinel* office. Somebody important, sounds like. Editor or something. Hasn't come through here yet. Called the captain at home, apparently. You and Cook. I got Tony, and he's on his way down. Captain Weigand said to have a cruiser pick you up, Lieutenant."

Shapiro said, "O.K., Sanders," and hung up and sat regarding the telephone and drinking coffee.

Somebody killed at a newspaper office; at the office of the only full-size afternoon newspaper remaining in the city of New York. And another world in which Shapiro would find himself entirely alien. Religious revivalists, advertising men, the world of book publishing. Trust Bill Weigand to find an assignment for Lieutenant Nathan Shapiro in an area about which Shapiro knew nothing. Hell, he didn't even read the *Sentinel*. The *Chronicle*, yes. Everybody had to read the *Chronicle*. Not to find out what had happened. TV took care of that. To relate what happened during one day to what had happened the day before, the year before. And to try to make sense of the composite. Which, on the whole, didn't seem often to add to sense.

"Whatever it is, you've got to eat breakfast," Rose said. "I've put the eggs on the coffee table. You've *got* to eat."

Nathan went to the sofa by the coffee table and sat on it and looked at scrambled eggs and triangles of toast. Rose brought his coffee cup and refilled it.

"While they're hot," Rose told him. "Warm, anyway."

Shapiro ate scrambled eggs and a few bites of toast. Rose joined him on the sofa. Her egg was soft-boiled.

"Somebody's been killed at the *Sentinel*," he told her. "The newspaper."

"Yes, dear," Rose Shapiro said. "I know the *Sentinel* is a newspaper. It has been for years. A hundred years or thereabouts, at a guess. Judging by its policies, which are pretty antique."

Shapiro shook a cigarette from a half-filled pack and was told he hadn't finished his eggs. He took a token bite. He nibbled at toast. Duty performed, he lighted his cigarette. He said, "You read the *Sentinel*, Rose?"

"Not much, these days. I used to. Oh, years ago. When it was, you might say, in its prime. Perhaps when I was."

He turned toward her and smiled and shook his head. "Consider it said," Nathan Shapiro told his wife.

She raised dark eyebrows at him. He merely looked at her, still smiling, still shaking his head.

"Oh, all right," Rose said. "It's foolish to fish in the morning. About the *Sentinel*—"

"And unnecessary, dear," Nathan said. "I thought last night would have—" He did not finish. He shook a cigarette loose and held the pack toward her. She took the cigarette and the flame of the lighter he held out for her.

"They know who's been killed at the paper, Nathan?"

"Sanders doesn't. Thinks it's somebody important. Like an editor or something. I suppose Bill knows. They're having a precinct cruiser pick me up."

"Then you'd better get dressed. And your good suit is back from the cleaners, remember. Although for the *Sentinel*

I suppose it ought to be a morning coat. *And* striped trousers."

"Like that?"

"Very dignified, I'd think. Maybe fuddy-duddy. But I merely glance at it now and then. It thinks the income tax is ruining the country. And that social security is part of the Communist conspiracy."

"Really, Rose?"

"Oh, not quite, I suppose. Something along those lines. You'd better get dressed, dear."

Shapiro got dressed. Since it was clear he was venturing among Republicans, he did put on the suit just back from the cleaners. It was a gray suit, and there were creases in the trousers. The creases differentiated it from the suit he had worn while walking Cleo. He strapped on the shoulder holster with the gun in it. He buttoned his jacket over the gun. The jacket hung loose on his long, spare frame. It did cover the gun. He did not suppose he would have to shoot his way into the offices of the New York *Sentinel*. Regulations required the sidearm.

He was back in the living room, where Rose was finishing a cigarette and sipping coffee, in time to assure a fractured voice on the lobby-to-apartment telephone that he was on his way down.

"Be careful, Nathan," Rose said, after he had kissed her. "Try to be home for dinner."

She did not sound optimistic about the last. Nathan said, "Sure," but there was no special confidence in his voice. As he opened the apartment door, Cleo arrived from the kitchen, leash in mouth. A foot gently persuaded her. She dropped the leash and made a small sound which was a little like a sob. Nathan told her he was sorry and went down the stairs.

The police car at the curb had two uniformed patrolmen in it. As Shapiro crossed the sidewalk, the one in the passenger seat got out and stood, more or less, at attention. He said, "Lieutenant Shapiro?" and, with that confirmed, "Good morning, Lieutenant."

Shapiro got in beside the driver, and the other patrolman got into the back of the car, where there were no inner handles on either door.

"Manhattan, they say," the driver said. "Newspaper building, they say. Sentinel Building. Broadway, block below Canal. That right, Lieutenant?"

"Whatever they told you," Shapiro said.

"Funny place for a newspaper," the driver said, and started the car toward Manhattan.

"A lot of them used to be downtown," Shapiro told the patrolman, who was obviously too young to know about that, or even that there had once been a lot of them. Shapiro himself was just old enough to have seen most of New York's newspapers wither and vanish.

The driver took the Manhattan Bridge. He made the mistake of continuing west on Canal Street, which was already traffic-jammed. What, Shapiro vaguely wondered, had ever happened to the notion of making Canal a depressed—or elevated—throughway bisecting Manhattan Island?

They inched through to Broadway. The Sentinel Building was a block downtown. It was a brick building, six stories tall. It looked to be a very old building. Rose's guess of a hundred years seemed plausible. A large clock, with "The New York Sentinel" in Old English letters on a plaque above it, stuck out from the brick facade. The clock, by Nathan's watch, was forty-two minutes slow.

The building occupied the block. On the downtown cross street, half a dozen trucks waited along the curb. Waiting to be loaded with newspapers? Shapiro wondered. But the *Sentinel* was an *afternoon* paper; it was not yet nine o'clock in the morning. The first of what Shapiro assumed would be numerous bewilderments. Did Captain William Weigand, commanding, Homicide, Manhattan South, arrange these things by intention?

The driver pulled the Brooklyn patrol car in behind two others, parked against the Broadway curb behind a black, unmarked sedan with only numbers on its license plate to reveal its identity as a car from the precinct detective squad.

The driver of the Brooklyn car said, "Need us anymore, Lieutenant?" Shapiro said he didn't and crossed the sidewalk to the entrance of the old brick building. He went through a revolving door under a wide sign with "The New York Sentinel" spelled out on it in somewhat tarnished metal letters, which were also in the Old English shape. He swirled out of the door into a big lobby, with two elevators on the far side of it. On his left were two large doors with frosted glass panels. On one of them was lettered "The New York Sentinel" and, below that announcement, "Business Office." The last was in modern lettering.

At the right side of the lobby there was a single door. There was an electric sign over it. The sign read "MacFarland's Pharmacy."

There was a uniformed patrolman in front of the elevators, neither of which appeared to be at ground level. Shapiro identified himself to the patrolman, who said, "Yes, Lieutenant. Second floor. Stairs right over there, sir."

He pointed to a door at one side of the elevators. Shapiro opened the door and climbed a flight of stairs—a rather long flight. Ceilings had been higher when the old building was put up. He came out into a wide corridor. He faced an arrow on the wall pointing to "Enquiries." But, just left of the top of the stairway, there was a wide opening in the wall, wide enough for double doors but with no doors in it. Typewriters were rattling beyond the opening. Also a voice, rather raised, and sounding impatient, came out into the corridor. The impatient word was *"Copy!"*

Shapiro went from the corridor into a big room with some twenty desks, about half of them occupied, arranged in rows. Men were typing at most of the occupied desks; a woman was at one of them. She was talking on a telephone and penciling notes on rather gray paper as she talked and listened. A man at one of the desks had earphones on and was typing what he heard through them. As Shapiro stepped into the big room, the man with the earphones tore the sheet out of his typewriter and said "Copy!" loudly and in an aggrieved voice. A boy of about sixteen went to him and took the sheet of paper held out and carried it a few steps to the middle of the room, to a semicircular table, with six men sitting around its rim. A seventh man sat, solitaire, in the hollow of the semicircle. One of the men on the rim wore an eyeshade. It was he who got the sheet from the typewriter of the man with the earphones.

A tall, youngish man came across the room from the direction of a desk under a window in the room's distant corner and from a gray-haired man sitting there reading a newspaper. The tall man said, "Morning, sir," to Nathan Shapiro. Shapiro said, "Morning, Tony," to Detective (1st gr.) Anthony Cook.

"Got here a while ago," Tony said. "They tell you who got killed, Nate?"

Shapiro shook his head. "The captain just had a car pick me up," he said. "Nobody's filled me in. S.O.S. didn't know." Detective Sanders's full name is Samuel Oscar Sanders.

"The voice of God," Tony Cook said. "That's who got killed. The voice of President McKinley, anyway. The man to the right of God, they've called him. Roger Claye." He stopped and looked at Shapiro, who felt he was supposed to jump. Instead, he merely raised his eyebrows.

"The columnist," Tony Cook said. "Monday, Wednesday and Friday. Syndicated all over the country. Still thinks Nixon was a great man, betrayed by little Democrats. And the elite Eastern establishment and the liberal media. Says it three times a week. And that there's a conservative swell throughout the country. And—you mean you've never read him, Nate?"

"I don't read the *Sentinel* much, Tony."

"He's all over the country," Tony said. "The Midwestern papers think he preaches the gospel. Rachel reads him.

Says it stimulates the adrenalin. When it doesn't make her throw up."

"Well," Shapiro said, "I'm just a nonpolitical cop. How is Rachel, by the way?"

Rachel was fine. Had been last night, anyway. And how was Rose?

Rose was a doctor of philosophy, as of two days ago. She was also fine.

"This man Claye," Shapiro said. "Killed here at the office?"

"Not here in the city room," Tony said. "Didn't show up here often, way I get it. In his own office other end of this floor. Didn't show up there much either, apparently. Mostly sent his columns in by messenger. Usually in the afternoons, they tell me."

Shapiro said, "Mmm." He said, "So this is the city room. I'd have thought it would be more—" He paused.

"Yeah," Tony said. "I saw the revival of *Front Page* too, Nate. Maybe things were like that, long time ago. In Chicago. Hiding escaped murderers in rolltop desks. Yelling all over the place. Quieter now. Was a good while back, too."

Nathan Shapiro raised his eyebrows again.

"Oh," Tony Cook said, "way back when I was about fifteen, I—"

Simultaneous loud cries of "Copy!" from several desks interrupted him. A youth of around sixteen hurried to one of the callers; a girl of about the same age went to another.

"—worked one summer as a copyboy," Tony Cook said. "Had a notion of being a newspaperman. The summer cured me. All the reporters beefing about their salaries. Talking about getting out of the racket and into advertising. So I decided to be a cop, way Dad was. Even that long ago, the city room I worked in wasn't a bedlam. Nobody was much rushing around in a frenzy. Pretty much the way it is here right now. And what they call the Home Edition closes in about"—he looked at his watch—"twenty-five minutes," he said.

"Also," Tony added, "I never found any bodies, way a kid on the lobster did this morning. Shock to the boy. Lost his breakfast."

"Claye's body?" Shapiro said. "On the what, Tony?"

"Only body we have," Tony Cook said. "Lobster trick. What they call it. Afternoon papers start around three in the morning. Three or four copyreaders and a slot man, except they call him an assistant city editor, come in then and send overnight copy out to the composing room. And a couple of reporters come in and rewrite stories from the morning papers. All stuff for the inside pages, of course. Play reviews, music reviews, that sort of thing. Movie reviews. And, part of the time, Claye's column. Usually, it gets down in time for the afternoon desk to handle. And Sampson to look it over, he tells me."

"Sampson?"

"Managing editor. Guy over there in the corner, reading this morning's *Chronicle*. Runs the news side. Alabama native, from what I hear. Deep South somewhere, anyway. Reads Claye's column in advance to see that no liberal tinge shows up. What Rachel told me once, anyway."

"Rachel, Tony?"

"Used to know a man who worked here. Music critic, assistant music critic. Something like that. Sampson fired him. The *Sentinel* was cutting down on music coverage about then. Because there wasn't enough advertising to make it worthwhile. Also, most of the people who read music reviews were—"

He stopped abruptly.

"The precinct boys went along through there," Tony said. "Where they found the body." He was pointing to an opening in the middle of the wall at their left. "And they've taken the early-trick assistant city editor to an office over there to talk to him. Maybe we ought to see what they've come up with, huh?"

Nathan Shapiro agreed they might as well. He was

mildly amused at Tony Cook's unexpected lapse into flagrant tact. It is, of course, quite true that many Jews are deeply responsive to music. And that they write a large percentage of it.

"Right through here," Tony said, and led the way through there. It was along a corridor, and from another doorless room to their right there was a clicking racket, like that of a dozen typewriters being hammered by typists with heavy hands.

"Ticker room," Tony said. "Associated Press, UPI, AP local."

There was a copyboy in the ticker room. He was tearing lengths of paper from one of the rapidly typing, unattended machines.

The short corridor ended in an area as large as the city room they had left. Originally, Shapiro guessed, it had been a room as open as that one. Offices had been partitioned off on both sides and at the end. There were two offices at the end of the room, and the door of one of them stood open. Detective Captain Callahan, commanding the precinct squad, stood in the open doorway, his back to the outer room. He was talking to somebody in the office. The door to one of the side offices was also open. A uniformed patrolman stood outside it. Four men were inside. One of them was using a camera; another was making a sketch of the room. Two lab men were dusting for prints.

"Took the body away several hours ago," Tony said. "Call went in to the precinct about four thirty."

It had taken a time for word to reach Homicide, Shapiro thought. Precinct had probably hoped to wrap it up unaided. Precinct squads cooperate with Homicide, but sometimes at arm's length. Homicide squad men are often referred to as "the brains," no compliment being intended.

Callahan turned to face them as they walked toward him. He said, "Oh." Then he said, "Morning, Nathan. You're sure as hell welcome to it."

Shapiro said, "Good morning, Captain. Want to fill us in?"

"With what we've got," Callahan said. "Which isn't one hell of a lot. Man named Claye got cooled. But plenty. Seems he wrote a column. Shot once. Middle of the forehead. In his office down there, where—way I get it—he wasn't really supposed to be. Some time around midnight, probably. But, seems like, nobody heard the shot. But you may as well get it from Mr. Parker here."

Callahan stepped aside, and Shapiro and Cook went into the office. It was reasonably large and had a floor-to-ceiling window through which bright sunlight was slanting.

"Mr. George Parker," Callahan said. "Lieutenant Shapiro, Mr. Parker. And Detective—"

Tony Cook supplied his name, which Callahan repeated to the slight, largely bald man who was sitting behind a desk too big for him. Parker looked worried. He was sweating perceptibly, although it was not especially warm in the room. Of course, he was sitting partly in the slanting morning sun.

Shapiro said, "Good morning, Mr. Parker," and waited.

"Look," Parker said. He had a small voice, one appropriate to his size. "I've been over it twice already. First this lieutenant who got here around five this morning, and then to Captain Callahan here. And it's not worth all that much."

"I know," Shapiro said. "We repeat ourselves, make other people repeat themselves. Just the way the routine is, Mr. Parker. Have to ask you to go over it again, I'm afraid."

Parker sighed. He said, "All right. I'm an assistant city editor. Early trick. Only it's more a slot man, really. Catch the overnights, check the mornings and have one of the boys follow up. Unless it's page one stuff, that is. Check on the services. Read copy. Send stuff along to the composing room. Sort of—oh, sweep up yesterday, if you know what I mean. See we're not missing out on anything. See what I mean?"

"I guess so," Shapiro said. "This morning, Mr. Parker. Wasn't like the usual morning, obviously."

Parker said it sure as hell wasn't.

He had come in at three in the morning, which was his regular time. He had been the first of the lobster crew. He usually was. There were two copyreaders with him on the early shift, and two reporters. To get started on the A.M.'s rewrite. While he waited for the others, he had gone over the copy already on the copydesk. Collier, Eugene Collier, the drama critic, had got his copy in all right. "Always go over that myself. Sometimes Gene gets in words Mr. Sampson doesn't like. Used 'scatological' one time. Boss Sampson pretty much went through the ceiling. Thought it was a dirty word."

"This morning?" Shapiro said.

The movie review copy was in. The *Sentinel* was exposing abuses in social welfare. Copy on that, the third installment, was in proof. What wasn't in either typescript *or* proof was Roger Claye's Friday column, "News in Perspective."

Usually, Claye got his copy to the office on the afternoon before it was to be printed. After being read and sent by the late-afternoon copydesk to be typeset, it was proofed up and on managing editor Sampson's desk in the city room when Sampson came in, usually about eight A.M. And proofs were also at the copydesk when Parker came in. Now and then, but rarely, only the copy from Claye's typewriter was there, waiting to be read and set in type.

This morning there had been neither copy nor proof. And there was no proof in the composing room. Parker had sent Ted there to check. Theodore Simon, that was. The copyboy working the lobster trick.

Parker had waited until almost four before he had done anything about it. Once in a while—"once in a blue moon"—Claye got his copy in late, sending it down by messenger. When it was three fifty-five—about then, anyway—Parker had decided he'd better check with Claye. "Although it was a hell of a time to be calling him up. He's a big shot around here, Lieutenant."

The small assistant city editor had nerved himself and

dialed the number of Claye's house. "What they call a town house, Lieutenant. On West Eleventh, I think it is. Never been there, of course."

He had let Claye's telephone ring a dozen times before he accepted that he was not going to get an answer; that there was nobody at the Claye house to answer. "There's a Mrs. Claye, but apparently she wasn't home, either." And if there were living-in servants, they obviously weren't going to answer telephones at four o'clock in the morning.

But there would be hell to pay if there was no Claye column in Friday's *Sentinel*, and none to mail out or to send out on leased wire to the syndicate's subscribers.

There was one last chance, and a faint one. Claye might, for some unguessable reason, have decided to come down to his office and write his column there. He never had before. Actually, as far as Parker knew, Claye almost never came to his office. Still—

"I sent the kid back to have a look. Just on a million-to-one chance." The kid was Ted Simon.

Roger Claye was in his office. He was sitting in a high-backed chair at his desk. There was a hole in the middle of his forehead and dried blood down the front of his clothes and on the top of the desk.

Theodore Simon had run back to Parker's desk in the city room and reported what he had seen. Then he had run out of the city room and down a corridor to the men's room.

He had still been there when the first patrolman had arrived.

"Lieutenant Daley sent him home," Callahan said. "He was one sick kid. Still being sick when Joe Daley got here."

2

Lieutenant Joseph Daley, who had had the midnight-to-eight shift at the precinct squad room, had sent the shaken copyboy home in a police car. Young Simon lived with his parents in the West Twenties.

Daley hadn't thought of many questions to ask the boy who had found a dead man sitting at his desk, still partly upright, with a hole in his head and blood all over him. Yes, the door to Claye's office had been closed. No, it had not been locked. Ted Simon had knocked on the closed door before he opened it, although he hadn't really expected anybody would be in the office. He had opened the door and seen who was.

Ted, when he had told Daley that, had had to back into a cubicle and vomit again. Then Daley had arranged for him to be taken home.

"Nothing to show there was anything thrown around in the office," Callahan told Shapiro and Cook. "What I mean is, no struggle. Looks like Claye just sat there and waited to be shot. By—the way it looks—somebody sitting across the desk from him. Sometime between midnight and one A.M., at a guess. The assistant M.E.'s guess, that is."

That was right. Of course, the city room was separated from these offices by the corridor with the ticker room off it. And the tickers made quite a racket. Yeah, sure, the tickers ran all night.

"I guess that's about all we have to ask you now, Mr. Parker," Shapiro said. "Right, Captain?"

"Far's I'm concerned," Callahan said. "Anyway, I'll see if the boys at Claye's office have turned up anything."

Callahan went out of the office and down the corridor toward the city room. Parker stood up behind the desk. He looked at Nathan Shapiro.

"Yes, Mr. Parker," Shapiro said. "You can go along home, if you want to. We know where you live, don't we?"

"In Queens," Parker said. "Yeah, one of them wrote my address down." He came around the desk and stepped toward the office door.

"One other thing," Shapiro said. "Mr. Claye wouldn't have had to go through the city room to get in here? Not that there was anybody around when he did come in, apparently."

Claye would not have had to go through the present city room to get to his office.

"Present?"

"The *Sentinel* used to be a morning paper," Parker said. "Fifteen or twenty years ago. And what's the *Sentinel* now was the *Evening Sentinel*. Long way back. Back when the old man owned them both. Before my time, Lieutenant."

"The old man, Mr. Parker?"

"Mr. Lester Mason. Bought the *Sentinel* in the early part of the century. Began buying other papers, too. Merged them with the *Sentinel*. What I meant was, this whole group of offices used to be one big room—the city room of the morning paper. He sold that, though."

Shapiro said he saw. He watched Parker walk away. He was as small walking as he had been sitting down. He walked toward the city room.

And then the building began to tremble a little. To vibrate. And from somewhere there was a muffled sound.

"It's all right," Tony said, when Shapiro looked at him. "Just the presses, Nate. In the basement. They've started to roll them."

Shapiro nodded his understanding. He said, "Want to check out on the other men who were on this early trick with Parker, Tony? Not that we're not probably getting it straight from Parker, but still. Callahan's probably got them cooped up somewhere."

Cook said, "Sure," and started out the door. He just missed collision with a man coming briskly in. Cook said, "Sorry." The newcomer didn't say anything. He came on into the office and looked hard at Nathan Shapiro.

He was, at a guess, in his middle forties. He was an inch or so shorter than Shapiro, which made him about six feet tall. He was compactly built; he had dark brown hair, cut a little shorter than was then the mode. He had a lean, intelligent face, deeply tanned. He looked to Shapiro like a man who probably played tennis a lot.

"You're another of them, I take it," the man said. He did not wait for comment, but went past Shapiro and sat behind the desk. It was clear that it was his desk.

"If you mean policemen," Shapiro said. "Yes, I am, Mr.—"

"Simms. Peter Simms. Associate editor. You people are all over the place, aren't you?"

"Pretty much, I guess," Shapiro said, and added his name and rank. "Thing like this does bring us out, Mr. Simms."

Simms agreed that it sure as hell did. He said it with a faint smile. Then he sobered. "It's a damn bad thing, Lieutenant," he said. "Bad for the *Sentinel*. Bad for a lot of people, probably. Republicans especially, of course. Probably left-wing terrorists did it. And I quote Roy Sampson, although I don't know if he's had a chance to say it yet. Claye was quite a guy, Shapiro. Any way you looked at it."

There was, Shapiro thought, the implication that there had been more than one way of looking at the late Roger Claye. He pulled a chair up and sat on the other side of Simms's desk. He said, "Associate editor, Mr. Simms?"

"What it says on the masthead. Russel Perryman, owner and publisher, Jason Wainwright, editor. Peter Simms, associate editor. Wainwright and I are supposed to set the policy, as reflected in the editorial articles. Carry it out is more like it. Perryman sets it. After all, it's his newspaper. He's the one hired Claye. And Roy Sampson, come to that. Who sees that our news stories have the right approach. Anything else you want to know, Shapiro?"

The faint smile was back, on lips and in voice.

"Primarily," Shapiro said, "who killed Mr. Claye. Any idea who might have wanted to, Mr. Simms?"

"Possibly a tenth of the population of the country," Simms said. "Oh, I don't mean actually kill him. Just somehow to get him to stop writing. You read his column, Lieutenant?"

Shapiro shook his head.

"Strange," Simms said. "The sixth floor thinks everybody does."

"The sixth floor, Mr. Simms?"

"The old man. Mr. Russel Perryman, owner and publisher. He has his offices on the sixth floor. On high, as it were. From whence all edicts flow. Like, Richard Nixon will go down in history as one of the nation's greatest presidents. Yes, still, Lieutenant. And I quote from last Monday's Roger Claye's column, Roger having been the anointed prophet."

Shapiro merely raised his eyebrows.

"Sound a little flippant, you think, Lieutenant? Perhaps

I do. What it comes down to, I'm a newspaperman." He said this as if it were a total explanation of something.

Simms watched Shapiro's face.

"Skip it, Lieutenant," he said. "We're all a little edgy this morning. Got me out of bed about six. Probably got everybody out about then."

Shapiro could only guess what he was supposed to skip. If he was skipping anything important, he could always come back and look for it.

"You were home at six?" Shapiro said.

Simms's smile grew wider. It seemed about to turn into open laughter.

"At home and in bed, Lieutenant. And asleep. With my wife in the bed next to mine. And our daughter, who is six years old and named Phyllis, in her room. Also asleep. And our apartment is in Brooklyn Heights, and Captain Callahan, or one of his boys, has the exact address. And I was there all night. Lieutenant. And asleep from about eleven until the phone rang. And, no, I didn't take time out to come over here and shoot Claye. Anything else, Lieutenant?"

"That about covers it," Shapiro said. "Is there a guard on here at nights, Mr. Simms? Somebody to check people in and out?"

"Could be. You'll have to ask the man who runs the building. The superintendent. I don't come over here much at nights. Don't ever, far's I can remember. No night work this end of things."

"You're lucky," Shapiro told the man who did not seem, particularly, to be in mourning for his lost colleague. "Well—"

He started to stand up.

"Don't get me wrong," Simms said. "We'll help you any way we can. All of us. Want me to check out about a night guard?" He reached for the telephone on his desk.

The captain would have checked on that, Shapiro told him. And that he wouldn't, for now anyway, take up any more of Simms's time. He might want to talk to him again, of course. When they had got more into things.

Shapiro was turning toward the office door when it opened. A long-haired youth came in. He had a sheaf of newspapers under his arm. He took one out of it and put it on Simms's desk. He turned and started out.

"Give the lieutenant a copy," Simms said. The boy turned and looked at Nathan Shapiro.

"Yes, Homer, he's a policeman," Simms said.

Homer didn't say anything. He did give Shapiro a copy of the first edition, the Home Edition, of the *Sentinel*.

There was a streamer headline across the top of the front page. It read: SENTINEL COLUMNIST SLAIN AT OFFICE DESK.

There were subsequent headlines down the right-hand column; at the top, the type was arranged in an inverted pyramid.

ROGER CLAYE SHOT TO DEATH
AT SENTINEL OFFICE

Under that there was a single line:

Left Terrorists Suspected

Shapiro's eyes went down to the text of the article. He read:

> Roger Claye, renowned political columnist of The Sentinel, was shot to death in his office in the Sentinel Building in the early morning hours today. According to the police, he was shot once in the head as he sat at his desk, apparently by someone sitting opposite him.
>
> The crime, the police say, was committed between the hours of midnight and 3 A.M., when the first of the reportorial staff came on duty. The body was discovered at about 4 A.M. by a member of the early staff who had

been sent to discover why Mr. Claye's column, intended for today's Sentinel, had not reached the copydesk.

Mr. Claye's typescript for his Friday column had not yet been found when this edition of The Sentinel went to press. The column, widely acclaimed, customarily appears on the opposite-editorial page under the heading "News in Perspective" Mondays, Wednesdays and Fridays. It also appears in more than a hundred other newspapers throughout the United States and Canada.

Mr. Claye has long been noted for his impartial espousal of the conservative viewpoint in national and international affairs. The possibility that he was the victim of some left-wing activist is not ruled out by the police, working under the direction of Chief of Detectives Timothy J. O'Malley.

Trust Deputy Chief Inspector O'Malley to get his name in, Shapiro thought. Of course, everything all policemen wearing gold shields did was under O'Malley's supervision. Still—

He was interrupted in reading, and in his vagrant thoughts, by Simms's voice. Simms was talking on the telephone.

"Listen, Roy," Simms said. "What's this 'more than a hundred' business? Can't your boys get the figures? After all, it's our syndicate."

There was a rasping sound from the telephone. It went on for some seconds.

"All right," Simms said, "so they get in late and have to look up the current figures. So, it's a hundred and twenty-three in the Night Edition. And listen, Roy, isn't that 'renowned' laying it on a little . . . Oh, sure he was. But we haven't got him to sell anymore, pal. And this left-wing terrorists—all right, activists—where did the cops get that bit, Roy? I've got one of them in the office here with me now, and he hasn't told me anything along that line. A Lieutenant

Shapiro . . . Yes, I suppose he is, from the name. Want me to ask him? Oh, all right. But you brought it up . . . Yes, I know we do. But no more than we usually do. Nothing like we did during Watergate. All right, Roy. Only thing was, Mr. Perryman will be expecting exact figures. Yes, I know."

Simms hung up. He looked at Shapiro. "Roy Sampson," he said. "The managing editor."

"Yes, I know," Shapiro said. "And he wanted to know whether I'm Jewish. Next time he asks you, tell him yes, Mr. Simms. And that I'm the son of a rabbi, if he wants to know. You know we do what, Mr. Simms—as you told Mr. Sampson?"

"Oh," Simms said. "Nothing important, Lieutenant. Roy reminded me we get a good deal of hate mail about Claye. Left-wing nuts. That sort of thing."

"Threatening letters?"

"Some of them. Mostly just squawks. Nothing like what we got when I wrote an editorial article suggesting that perhaps some sort of gun registration might be conceivably useful if people went on killing presidents, or trying to. The gun boys swamped us on that, Lieutenant."

Shapiro didn't doubt the "gun boys" had. The rifle association regards the words "registration" and "confiscation" as synonymous. Or seeks to persuade members of Congress that they are. With, from Nathan Shapiro's point of view, unfortunate success. Policemen, like others, prefer to live.

Did Mr. Simms know whether any of the hate letters against Claye were around?

Simms doubted it. A few of the milder and more argumentative ones had been printed on the editorial page in the "Readers Speak" column. Most of them had gone into wastebaskets. "We get a good deal of mail from people who don't agree with us," Simms said. "We print a few of them. The *Sentinel* is an impartial, objective reporter of the world's events, Lieutenant."

Shapiro said, "Sure," with no inflection in his voice.

Simms smiled. There was, Shapiro thought, inflection in his smile. He said, "In the established tradition of journalism, end quote." There was a certain dryness in his soft, modulated voice.

"One thing is," Shapiro said, "how did these left-wing terrorists know Mr. Claye would be in his office here in the middle of the night? I gather that wasn't usual."

"No," Simms said. "Unprecedented is perhaps the word. Or, as a correspondent of ours in London once cabled, 'heretofore unprecedented.' I've no idea, Lieutenant. No reason I can think of why he would have been. Or how anybody could know he was going to be. Unless—"

"Yes," Shapiro said. "Unless he had an arrangement to meet somebody here."

Simms agreed that there was that. Shapiro thanked Simms for his time and stood up and turned again toward the door. It opened before he could reach it.

The man who came into Simms's office was tall—taller even than Shapiro himself. He wore a dark blue suit and a white shirt and a dark blue necktie. He was very thin under the suit. He had white hair, which was not as abundant as it probably once had been. His long, thin face was almost colorless, and a commanding nose jutted from it. He came into the office, Shapiro felt, as if he owned it. And Peter Simms stood up behind his desk.

Simms said, "Good morning, sir."

The white-haired man did not appear to hear this. He looked at Shapiro. He said, "Who's this, Simms?" He had a cold voice.

"He's a police officer, Mr. Perryman," Simms said. "A lieutenant from the Homicide Squad. A Lieutenant Shapiro."

"A lieutenant, eh?" Perryman said. "Shapiro, eh? Where's the inspector, Shapiro? O'Malley, isn't it?"

"Probably at headquarters," Shapiro told him. "The squad does the spadework, Mr. Perryman. Anything we find out is passed on to the chief, of course."

"Yeah? And what do you expect to spade up here, Shapiro? And where's your superior officer? Out rounding up the goddamn commies who did this, I hope."

"Captain Callahan is in the building," Shapiro said. "He's in command of the precinct detectives. Checking things out with some of his men. There are quite a few of us here, Mr. Perryman."

"Messing around with it," Perryman said. "Nobody here killed Claye. One of those goddamn radicals. Commie, obviously. Sticks out a mile. You can see that, can't you—and this Callahan? If you can't, the commissioner will. He owes me that much—at least that much. Law-and-order man, that's what Pierce is. Crack down on these murdering commies, Pierce will."

"We all try to crack down on murderers," Shapiro said.

"And don't have much luck, do you, Shapiro? Our goddamn Supreme Court sees to that. Simms!"

Peter Simms was still standing behind his desk. He said, "Sir?"

"Want an editorial for the next edition. Tragic event, great loss to the nation. That sort of thing. Example of the breakdown of law and order. You'll know what to say. And no beating around the bush, Simms. Lay it on them, is what I mean. Understood, Simms?"

"Yes, sir. You want me to write it, Mr. Perryman? Not Mr. Wainwright?"

"You, Simms. Old Wainwright's slowing down. You know that as well as I do. Not the man he used to be. You've got it clear, Simms? Lead the page and set two columns. And no pussyfooting. You understand? And I'll want to see it before it goes in. Get that?"

Simms said, "Yes, Mr. Perryman. I'll get right on it. Have to junk some stuff to get it in. Rather long article about college professors who oppose the free enterprise system."

"Junk it if you have to," Russel Perryman said, and went out of the office. Even from the rear, Shapiro thought, he looked the owner and publisher of the New York *Sentinel*. No wonder he had come into Simms's office as if he owned it. He did.

Simms said "Whew!" and sat down behind his desk. He swiveled in his chair and drew a typewriter table up so that he faced a somewhat battered Underwood. He fed paper into the machine, then leaned back in his chair and stared at it.

"A very authoritative man, Mr. Perryman," Shapiro said.

Simms said, "Uh," and leaned forward and began to pound the typewriter.

Shapiro went out to look for Callahan and, of course, Detective Cook.

3

SHAPIRO found Callahan and Cook in the wide hallway outside the office which had been Roger Claye's. Callahan was talking to a man who was making notes on folded sheets of copy paper.

"Yes," Callahan told the man, "we have found fingerprints. Including Mr. Claye's, of course. And a good many others. Not very recent, for the most part. Some may be."

"You don't know whose they are, Captain?"

"They'll be classified and checked out, in the usual way, Mr. Notson. In Washington, if necessary."

"Among the prints of known subversives? That the FBI has?"

"Prints of everybody on file, of course. Ours here at headquarters. The armed forces in Washington. The FBI and the CIA. Everybody who has files of fingerprints. It takes a little while, of course."

"The bullet, Captain?"

"We don't know yet. Probably small-caliber, from what the officers saw before the body was taken to the morgue. The autopsy findings won't come through until this afternoon."

"And the bullet—just one, from what we get—will be compared with—"

"When we find something to compare it with," Callahan said. "Yes, apparently just one slug, Mr. Notson. This is Mr. Notson. One of the reporters. This is Lieutenant Shapiro, Mr. Notson. From Homicide."

"Jim Notson, Lieutenant. I'm doing a rewrite for the Night. Anything you can tell us?"

"Nothing the captain hasn't already told you," Shapiro said. "We'll give you more when we have more. For now, you'll have to go on what you have."

"Or can dig up, Lieutenant."

"Or can dig up, of course. And if you do dig up anything, we'll want to know about it."

James Notson, *Sentinel* reporter, said, "Sure," and went down the corridor to the city room.

"Trouble is, Nate," Callahan said, "you're pretty much asking them to get underfoot."

"They would anyway," Shapiro said. "And the boys from the *Post* and the *News* and the *Chronicle* and from all the networks. Sure they'll get underfoot. No way of stopping them. Or the services."

"Or the local TV news boys," Tony Cook said. "And—hell—everybody."

Shapiro nodded his agreement. He was going to turn up in the middle of a big one. Big and confusing and not at all his line of country. Thanks to Bill Weigand, who could never understand the limitations of Lieutenant Nathan Shapiro. Just because I'm lucky sometimes, Nathan Shapiro thought.

"What do we know about security here, Captain?" he asked. "Night security?"

"Doesn't seem to be much," Callahan said. "Oh, a night

watchman. Who covers all six floors and rings in every hour or so. Watching out for fires, mostly."

"Nobody in the lobby, checking people in and out?"

"Building superintendent says not. Man named Folsom, he is. Says there used to be, couple of years ago, but he was told to fire him. Costing too much money, he thinks. And the elevators are shut down at seven in the evening. Start up again around nine in the morning. Way to save energy, Folsom says. What they told him, anyway. Very strong on saving energy, the *Sentinel* is. While back there, they had WIN painted every day in what they call an ear. Weather report in one ear and WIN in the other. You remember the WIN gimmick, Nate?"

Shapiro remembered the WIN gimmick, so triumphantly launched and so quickly submerged early in the Ford administration.

"So anybody who comes in at night has to walk up the stairs?" he said.

"Staff's supposed to anyway, they tell me. Editorial staff, that is. Everybody who works on the second floor, anyway. Editorial people and the composing-room people. The pressmen have their own entrance to the pressroom. It's in the basement."

"So anybody can just walk in and go up the stairs and wherever he wants to go. And if he wants to kill Claye, just find Claye's office and pull a trigger?"

"What it adds up to, Nate. Just have to find Claye's office and find Claye in it."

"Which," Shapiro said, "it appears he wasn't often."

"Way it looks, Nate. We don't know much about him, do we? Except he's dead."

"That, and that he was 'renowned.' Says so in the paper. See that, Captain?"

Captain Callahan had seen that. He had also seen, under a flash after the main account of Roger Claye's murder, an account of his life.

"Seems he was a great guy," Callahan said. "'A moving force for sanity in American life.' Also, 'A life-long advocate of fiscal responsibility at the federal level.'"

Nathan Shapiro had not got that far into Roger Claye's obituary notice. It had looked like being rather long. He mentioned this estimate to Callahan.

"Well," Callahan said, "he was their great man, Nate. Their fair-haired boy, apparently. Naturally, they'd be generous with their space."

"Yes. And maybe with their evaluation," Shapiro said. "Maybe there'll turn out to be a few things about him they don't stress. Something that might give us a hint as to why he got killed. The victim's past sometimes does that, you know."

"Sure. Like he was mixed up with the Mafia. Or had a police record that the *Sentinel*'s forgetting to mention. I'd better be getting back to the station house. Get some of the boys digging around. On this and, God knows, a dozen other things. With more coming in every minute. So?"

Nathan said, "Sure," and that he and Cook would see what else they could dig up. Here and at Claye's town house, if anybody had turned up at the town house. In the Village, wasn't it?

Callahan gave him the address, which was on West Eleventh Street, between Fifth Avenue and Sixth. And Callahan would be getting along for now. Then he got along, collecting detectives from the precinct squad to take with him, leaving uniformed patrolmen as symbols of police activity.

"There'll be clippings on Claye in the morgue," Cook said. "The newspaper morgue, I mean. And there's always *Who's Who*. Could be there's a copy at the city desk. Want I should—"

Shapiro did. Tony Cook went off toward the city room. Shapiro went into Claye's former office, although anything there would already have been scrutinized and fingerprinted. And, God knew, photographed.

The office was small and uncluttered. It held a desk and a typewriter on a stand. It had one small window, with an air shaft beyond it. There was a high-backed chair behind the desk, on which there was nothing except, propped between heavy glass bookstops, a dictionary and a copy of Fowler's *Modern English Usage,* revised edition. And there were bloodstains on the desk top and on the chair behind it. On the straight wooden chair that was set facing the desk on the visitor's side, there were traces of the powder the lab men had used.

The office looked somehow forsaken, as if nobody had ever sat in the high-backed desk chair, or tossed paper into the now empty wastebasket. Of course, the lab boys had emptied the wastebasket.

Shapiro leaned down and looked at the typewriter ribbon. It appeared to be an almost new ribbon, against which few keys had been struck. If Claye had come to his office to write his Friday column, it had been a very short column. Or written longhand, for later copying?

If there had been anything revealing in this small office, it had been removed by the lab men. And anything possibly significant would show up at Homicide South. Along with the autopsy report and information from ballistics.

So. Shapiro left Claye's office, closing the door behind him. It did not, he noted, have a snap lock.

Tony Cook came along the corridor, carrying a thick book with folded paper marking a place in it.

"Yeah," Cook said. "He made it. Not that it's all that damn hard to make, from what I hear. This music critic Rachel knows, the one used to work here, signed a contract with a lecture agent, and all at once *Who's Who* tapped him."

They went into an empty small office two doors from the one Roger Claye had died in and equally without signs of recent use. At the desk, Shapiro opened *Who's Who in*

America at the page Cook had marked with folded copy paper. He read:

> Claye, Roger Arnold, political columnist; b. Des Moines, Iowa, August 3, 1920; s. Ernest and Emily (Foster) C.; A.B. cum laude, Iowa University, 1940; m. Gertrude Finney, June 21, 1941 (dec. May 1947); m. 2d, Faith Bradford, April 14, 1962. Public relations, Des Moines Chamber of Commerce, 1940–41; public relations staff National Association of Manufacturers, 1942–56; political columnist, New York Sentinel, 1962; syndicated 1964–. Mem. U.S. Chamber of Commerce, Rotary, John Birch Society. Author: The Engulfing Wave, 1958; Our Endangered Liberties, 1962. Home: Bedford Hills NY 10507.

"West Eleventh Street not mentioned," Tony Cook said, when Shapiro had finished reading. "I think that means Bedford Hills is their legal residence—not that it matters, probably."

Shapiro said, "Mmm," and reread Roger Arnold Claye's biography. A considerable employment hole in it, he thought. What had Claye been doing between 1956 and 1962? Working on a newspaper? Or merely writing books about engulfing waves and threats to liberty?

Married twice, the first time when he was twenty-one. To one Gertrude Finney, presumably his age or younger and deceased, apparently, while still young. Claye had been in his forties when he married again. Gertrude had died, presumably, of natural causes. (It's part of my trade to wonder about that, Shapiro thought. Most people do die of natural causes. No reason to think Gertrude Finney Claye had not. No conceivable reason to grope into the distant past for a possible motive for retaliation. Many people die young, for many reasons.)

Faith Bradford the second wife. Faith had once been a

name not infrequently bestowed on female infants. (So had "Hope" and, for that matter, "Charity.") Not often used nowadays, so far as Nathan Shapiro knew. Bradford? It had a faintly New England feel about it. One thought, vaguely, of Cabots and Lowells. An old rhyme about them? One talked only with the other and the other only with God. Cabots with Lowells, or the other way around? Rose would know; it was the kind of thing on the tip of her mind.

Mine wanders, Shapiro thought. There was no special reason to wonder whether Bradfords had been on speaking terms with either ancient and celebrated family.

Of course, to let the mind wander further, the Bradfords might be an old New England family; it might be a family of high social and, perhaps, financial standing. A good family for an earnest young man from Iowa to marry into. So married, an aspiring man might well take time out to write books, without too much wondering how they would sell.

Member of the John Birch Society. And making no bones about it. As some, understandably to Nathan, did. Of the Klan, too?

"He left holes in it," Shapiro said. "Probably not important. Probably his wife can fill them in when we get around to her. Wonder if she's got home from wherever she's been? Wherever she was at four this morning, that is."

"Or," Tony said, "just not answering her telephone. Some people don't. Or up at this home of theirs in Bedford Hills. Captain Callahan's got the Eleventh Street house staked out."

Shapiro said, "Mmm."

"There'll be clippings about him in the morgue," Tony Cook said. "Want I should?"

Shapiro said, "Yes, Tony," and Cook went off to find the *Sentinel*'s morgue. He was gone about five minutes. He came back shaking his head. "Clips on Claye checked out," he said, "by James Notson. The reporter was talking to Callahan. Bringing the obit up to date. Maybe the managing editor can fill us in with what you want. Although probably he's busy as hell. This man Simms?"

"Simms is busy too," Shapiro said. "Writing an editorial about the breakdown of law and order."

"Well," Tony said, "we know Claye's dead."

"A man named Claye," Shapiro said. "A renowned columnist. Formerly a publicity man for the NAM. And a member of the John Birch Society."

"Gives us the feel of him," Tony said, and Shapiro agreed that it did.

"Of the surface of him, Tony," Shapiro said. "We could do with more. Let's see if Mr. Wainwright is too busy to talk to us. As long as we're here."

They went back along the corridor walled by the office doors to the two adjoining offices at the end of it. Through the door to Simms's office they could hear the clatter of typewriter keys. Simms was still writing a lament for the passing of Roger Claye—and, of course, the rule of law and order. Tony knocked on the door of the adjacent office. After a moment they heard, "Come in." The voice did not, as Shapiro had supposed it might, quaver. His voice, if it was Wainwright's, was not that of a man who was slowing down; was not what he had been. It was not a young voice, but it was a vigorous one. They went into the office.

It was about the size of Simms's adjacent office. A gray-haired man was sitting at a bare-topped desk, his back to a tall window through which the sun was shining. It shone on the thick gray hair of the man sitting behind the desk. Shapiro said, "Mr. Wainwright?" and the editor of the New York *Sentinel* said, "Yes." Shapiro told him who they were. Wainwright said, "So?"

"We're trying to get some background on Mr. Claye," Shapiro told him. "Something personal about him, if you know what I mean."

"I'm familiar with the English language," Wainwright said. "If you are, you can read about him in the next edition.

Read all about it, as they used to say. In the old days, when people got their news from newspapers."

Wainwright might be old. Shapiro guessed, from his lined, pale face, in his middle or late seventies. But there was still crackle in his voice. His hands moved still with quick precision.

"We'll read it," Shapiro said. "Sometimes there's more about a man than comes out in an obituary. Something, oh, between the lines."

"We'll give Roger Claye full coverage," Wainwright said. "What have you got in mind, Lieutenant?"

"Anything you can tell us. What kind of man was he, sir?"

The "sir" was more or less involuntary. But Shapiro felt it belonged there.

"Very able man," Wainwright said. "By today's standards. Can't you be more specific about what you want?"

"In his *Who's Who* entry," Shapiro said, "there seems to be a gap of several years. A gap in his activities. Oh, a couple of books published. But the period is a little more than five years. Researching for his books, Mr. Wainwright? Or working on newspapers? We like to know all we can find out about a victim's past, you see."

"On the chance it might have spilled over into the present?"

"Something like that, Mr. Wainwright. You see, at this stage of things, we have to grope around where we can."

"When was this period you find a gap in, Lieutenant?"

"Five-year period—1956 to 1962."

Wainwright shook his head. He said, "Afraid I can't help you. Oh, he wasn't working on a newspaper. Never did, actually. Did marry Faith Bradford along then. Wouldn't have needed to work at anything, I suppose. Maybe he just—coasted. And wrote those books. I've not read them, but I doubt if they needed much research. Think pieces, out of the top of his head, I imagine. Like the ones he's been doing for us."

"What do you mean, he never worked on a newspaper, sir? He worked for this one."

"Meant just what I said. He wasn't ever a newspaperman. Started out writing a column. Kept on writing a column. Think pieces."

"Oh," Shapiro said. "I'd always supposed columnists came up from being reporters. Or, maybe, editors of some kind."

"Or sportswriters," Wainwright said. "Like Broun. Pegler, for that matter. Yes, that's the usual progression. I don't know that 'up' is always the right word, Lieutenant. But let it ride. Thing is, Claye just—burst into bloom. No budding period. From press agent to seer in a single jump."

"Quite a jump," Shapiro said. He put a little emphasis on the word "quite," Wainwright's tone having encouraged it.

Wainwright smiled slightly. "It would seem so," he said. "Heretofore unprecedented."

The London correspondent's tautology, at cable press rates, seemed to be a lingering joke in the editorial department of the *Sentinel*.

"Possibly his marriage didn't hurt," Wainwright said, a little as if he were talking, reflectively, to himself. Shapiro waited, as he felt he was supposed to.

"Faith's father," Wainwright said, "was a business associate of the *Sentinel*'s present owner. Over a period of years, I believe. Roberts Bradford. Not Robert. Roberts with an 's.' Family name. He died a couple of years ago. Widower. One child, our Faith. What some people call a substantial man, Bradford was."

"He was a publisher?" Shapiro said. "Like Mr. Perryman?"

"Wholesale grocer," Wainwright said. "Our owner runs a chain of supermarkets. Before they were called supermarkets. Chain of grocery stores. He owns it. His and Bradford's interests—well, interlocked to a degree. Not particularly germane to your investigation, is it?"

"Probably not," Shapiro said. "Is what you mean, sir, that the Bradford-Perryman association may have given a certain impetus to Claye's jump? The hitherto unprecedented jump? When Claye and Faith got married?"

"Is it?" Wainwright said. "Mr. Claye was a very able man, Lieutenant. Probably didn't need what you call impetus."

Shapiro had not been questioning Claye's ability. He said so. Wainwright merely smiled and nodded his head.

"Mr. Perryman bought the *Sentinel*?" Shapiro said. "Quite a change from the retail grocery business, wasn't it?"

"About fifteen years ago," Wainwright said. "From old Lester Mason. You've heard of Mason, I suppose?"

"Not until Mr. Parker mentioned him."

Wainwright looked surprised. "Built the paper up to what it is," Wainwright said. "To what it was fifteen years ago, that is. Sold the morning paper. Then the *Evening Sentinel* became the *Sentinel*. Bought up three afternoons, and merged them. The *Sentinel-Observer, Sentinel-Express*. That sort of thing. Always boiled down to just the *Sentinel*, of course. Quite a newspaperman, old Mason was. In his way, which some people didn't like. Particularly those who were working on the absorbed papers, naturally."

Shapiro said he saw. He said, "You came to the *Sentinel* from one of these absorbed newspapers, Mr. Wainwright?"

"No, Lieutenant. Original *Sentinel* man. Oh, I've seen them come and go. Mostly go, the last few years. Variety of reasons. Radio and TV. Was a time the afternoons made a point of being on the street first with big stories. Now, who cares? The news is stale by the time we print it. And the big stores opening branches in the suburbs, because that's where their customers are going. And taking their advertising with them. Different fifty years ago—no, more than fifty. When I got my first job here, Lieutenant. As a cub, on the morning edition. Fifty-five years ago, damn near. I'm an old man, Shapiro. Should have retired years ago, some people think. Still, I like to stick around to see what happens. And, I've got a contract renewable at my option. A thing the present owner had to take over from old Mason. I'm talking quite a lot, I'm afraid. Wasting your time. And my own. Ought to be lining up the articles for tomorrow's page. And going over the stuff for the op-ed page, although that's really Pete Simms's job. I—yes, come in."

It was Peter Simms who had knocked—and came in.

"Piece on Claye," Simms said. "Sixth floor wants it for the night. And wants to read it over. Want you to vet it first, of course."

"Channels," Wainwright said, and took the typed sheets Simms held out to him. He started to read and then looked at Shapiro, who had got up from the wooden chair he had been sitting in.

Wainwright said, "I talk too much, Lieutenant. Without being of any help, I'm afraid."

Shapiro said he appreciated the time Wainwright had given him. He did not comment on the help Wainwright had, or had not, given him. He looked at Tony Cook, who had been making notes, and they both went out into the corridor.

4

One of the left-behind patrolmen had been looking for them, to deliver a message from the Claye stakeout, relayed through precinct. Mrs. Roger Claye had returned to the Eleventh Street town house. At least, a woman with a key to the house had returned to it, by cab, and had gone into it. The cab had driven off. One thing noticed; probably of no importance: the hacker had driven off with his flag still down. Nobody had got out of the cab except the woman who had a key to the house.

A cruise car took Shapiro and Tony Cook uptown to West Eleventh Street. The house was four stories tall and a little wider than those on either side of it. White stone steps led up from the sidewalk. They looked scrubbed. There was a polished brass rail on either side of the steps. They went up the steps and a heavy wooden door stopped them. There was no glass in the door. There was a button to push, and Tony pushed it. There was no sound of a bell through the solid, heavy door, but after they had waited for some seconds, the door opened. It opened on a chain.

The woman who had opened the door but not unchained it was slight and had auburn hair, hanging loosely to her shoulders. She looked, to Shapiro, to be in her early thirties. She was wearing a black suit, with a white blouse under the jacket. She said, "Yes?" She had a clear, quiet voice.

Shapiro said, "Mrs. Claye?" and when she nodded her head, soft hair swirling around it, "We're police officers, Mrs. Claye."

"Yes," she said. "I supposed you'd come. About this terrible thing that's happened. This—unbelievable thing." She unchained the heavy door and opened it. They went into a big entry hall, deeply carpeted, with a staircase rising out of it. The house faced south, and the morning September sunlight spilled through the open door from the east and brightened the deep orange carpet.

Shapiro felt that they should have carefully wiped their feet outside. And was glad that they would not have to break the news to Faith Claye. Radio, or perhaps morning TV, had done that for them.

A very pretty woman, he thought, as she led them into a long living room. She touched a switch, and table lamps went on in the room. The light was subdued; everything in the room was subdued—subdued and quiet and—elegant? So, for that matter, was Faith Claye herself. She was taking it well, Shapiro thought. When, inside the room, she faced them and motioned to deep chairs on either side of a wide fireplace, she did not look as if she had been crying. Her face was merely grave.

When Shapiro and Cook had sat in the chairs she indicated, she herself sat on a sofa facing the fireplace. Logs, which looked almost too perfect to be real, were arranged in the fireplace—ready for the dank cold of November. A very pretty woman, whatever her age, Shapiro thought again. Years younger than her husband had been, certainly.

"You've found out who did it?" she said, her voice still clear and quiet. "Who murdered my husband?" On the word "murdered," her voice caught, just perceptibly. "Is that what you've come to tell me?"

"No," Shapiro told her. "We haven't yet, Mrs. Claye. I'm Nathan Shapiro, by the way. A Homicide lieutenant. This is Detective Cook."

She nodded.

"Since you already know what happened," Shapiro said, "perhaps you can help us, Mrs. Claye."

She said she didn't know how she could, but that, of course, she would in any way she could. She said, "Would you like coffee or something, Lieutenant? Mr. Cook?"

Both shook their heads.

"I don't know why I said that," she said. "There's really nobody here to get us coffee. I'm not even sure there's coffee in the house. It's—well, still pretty much closed down for the summer. We'd planned to move back in a couple of weeks, but now—" She did not finish the sentence, let her voice trail off. She said, "How can I help you?"

"The usual things," Shapiro said. "Do you know if your husband had any enemies, Mrs. Claye?"

"Hundreds, I suppose. Thousands. But not the kind I guess you mean. Riffraff. Radicals who call themselves liberals. Want those of us who do things to support all those who won't. And people who want us not to spend anything for our own defense; want us to be left at the mercy of communism; of the people in the Soviet Union who are planning to take over the world. People like that hated Roger. Because of all he stood for."

She left no doubt where she stood, Shapiro thought. Probably he would have to look up and read some of her late husband's columns. Or perhaps he wouldn't need to.

Shapiro said he saw. He said that, of course, they would be looking into that angle.

"What I was thinking of," he said, "was personal enemies. Anybody who might have hated your husband as—well, as a man. Not merely disagreed with what he wrote. What, as you say, he stood for."

"No," she said, "I'm sure he didn't have any enemies of that kind. He would never have hurt anybody, not to make them hate him. Make them want to kill him. You'll find it was some terrorist—some crazy extremist—who did it, Lieutenant. I'm sure of that. Probably one of these kids who go around killing policemen and call themselves revolutionaries."

"We'll look for people like that," Shapiro told the auburn-haired woman, who had spoken intensely although without raising her voice; who had leaned toward him as she spoke and had clenched the fists in her lap. "Can you tell me something about your husband's activities yesterday, Mrs. Claye? Last night? How he happened to go down to his office at the newspaper in the middle of last night? An office, we're told, he didn't use much."

"Now and then he went there," she said. "When he wanted to look up something in their library—the morgue, I think they call it. Something for his column. I suppose that's why he went there last night. Uncle Russel doesn't have that building properly guarded. I've told him that often enough."

Uncle Russel? Of course—Russel Perryman, owner and publisher; "Uncle" a courtesy title.

"Did you know your husband was going down to the *Sentinel* last night, Mrs. Claye?"

"No, he didn't say anything about that. Only that he was tied up and not to expect him until morning. That would be this morning. But, as I said, he sometimes went down there at night to look things up. And sometimes, when we're back in town, to that poker game of theirs."

"Poker game?"

"Some of the men on the paper—some of the executives,

I mean—play poker once a week down there, and Roger sometimes sits in when we're in town."

"And he said not to expect him until this morning? Expect him where, Mrs. Claye?"

"At home, of course. Where we always are in the summers. Up until the middle of October, usually."

"Yes," Shapiro said. "And just where is that, Mrs. Claye?"

"In Bedford Hills. It's quiet and peaceful there, and much cooler than it is here in town. Roger always liked to work there. Of course, sometimes he could get up only on weekends. Thursdays, usually, after he had finished his Friday column and turned the copy in."

"But not this past Thursday?"

"No. There was something coming up. Breaking, he called it, that he wanted to comment on in his Friday piece. He always called them pieces, Lieutenant."

"It was yesterday he called you—I assume he called you—in Bedford Hills and told you he wouldn't get there until today?"

"Yes, Lieutenant. He calls me almost every evening when he's in town and I'm up there. Did, I mean. He won't anymore, will he?"

She put her face in her hands then, and sat so, bent forward, for some seconds. But when she straightened up again, it appeared to Shapiro that she was still dry-eyed.

"I'm sorry," she said. "I—I guess I'm still a little numb. Then, suddenly, it hits me."

"It happens that way lots of times," Shapiro said. "And I'm sorry we have to bother you just now. But sometimes we have to. I'm sure you understand."

"Of course," she said. "And I want to do everything I can to help. And it's really what Roger wrote so much about—the individual's part in maintaining law and order. I—I never dreamed I'd have a part in it. That it would come so close to me. But decent people don't, I guess. Think it stays miles away, among the dreadful radicals. And criminals, of course. Other criminals, I mean. Roger was always saying that; that it was up to ordinary, decent citizens to protect our society from those who want to destroy it, to tear it apart."

"Yes," Shapiro said. "Mr. Claye called you yesterday and said he had to stay in town. I suppose he would have stayed here, Mrs. Claye? Here in the house, I mean."

"No," she said. "The staff goes to the country with us. In early May, usually. This house is shut up for the summer. Oh, a man we hire stays here. Sleeps in a room downstairs to keep an eye on things; see the house isn't broken into. But there's nobody here to *do* things. Even to keep the air conditioning on. When he had to be in town during the summer, Roger stayed at the Plaza. My father used to keep rooms there, and now—until now, I mean—Roger used them when he had to be in town."

"I see," Shapiro said. "About when did Mr. Claye call, Mrs. Claye?"

"About five. Somewhere around then. When he usually called."

"And you stayed in Bedford Hills last night and drove in when—well, when you heard the news on the radio?"

"On TV, actually. At the Algonquin, when I was having breakfast. You see, I didn't stay in Bedford last night. I'd meant to and then—well, something came up. So I got a train into town. From White Plains. I had Luther drive me over to the station. Luther's our chauffeur, of course."

Many things seemed in the natural course of things to Faith Claye, Shapiro thought. Having a chauffeur, having houses both in the city and at Bedford Hills, along with a permanent suite at the Plaza. The sort of things, her "of course" implied, that everybody had.

"Do you mind telling us what this thing that came up was, Mrs. Claye? That made you change your plans and come into town?"

"Of course not. Why should I? A friend called and said

he'd managed to get seats to *Roundabout.* A play I've been simply dying to see. Like everybody else. So the only seats they have are for sometime in December. And dear Brian came up with house seats, Lieutenant. *House* seats. He's a playwright himself, of course. But it still seemed like a miracle. So, of course, I came right in. Who wouldn't have?"

Shapiro could think of several, including Rose and Nathan Shapiro. What he said was, "This Brian, Mrs. Claye? He was going with you to the theater, I suppose?"

"Of course. Brian Mead, the playwright. You must have heard of him."

Shapiro hadn't. Tony said, "I have, Mrs. Claye. He has two plays on Broadway just now, sir. Both hits."

Shapiro said, "Mmm." He said, "You got a train at White Plains and came into New York to meet Mr. Mead. And met him, I take it. And went to—"

"I don't see what this has to do with anything, Lieutenant. With my husband's death, which you're investigating." She added, "You say," and for the first time her voice sharpened.

"Nothing, probably," Shapiro said. "Nothing I can think of, anyway. They want us to get everything tied up. Insist on it, in fact. A nuisance for everybody, but there it is."

Nobody has ever asked Nathan Shapiro to identify the "they" to whom he is apt to pass responsibility. Which is perhaps as well.

"You did meet Mr. Mead, Mrs. Claye? Just for the record." He looked at Tony Cook, who was taking shorthand notes. Who, anyway, had better be. Not that their combined memories didn't usually suffice. Tony poised a pencil over folded sheets of paper which served as a notebook.

"Of course I met him," Faith Claye said. "At the Algonquin. Where he lives. And we had dinner there and went to see *Roundabout.* Will they want to know what we had for dinner, Lieutenant? And what I thought of the play?"

Shapiro smiled to show he realized the questions were rhetorical. He shook his head.

"I had their roast beef," Mrs. Claye said. "Rare, and it was very good. And I was a little disappointed in the play, Lieutenant. It's about a man who thinks he's a giraffe. And who gets lost in a traffic circle and keeps going round and round. And around. I don't think you'll really have to see it, Lieutenant."

Shapiro managed another smile. To show he wasn't missing anything, that he was with it.

"And after the theater, Mrs. Claye? You weren't in Bedford last night, I think you said."

"That's right. I'd planned to take the last train back, and Brian and I stopped by the Algonquin for—well, for a night-cap and a bite of supper. Before I caught the train. But then, just as I was ready to leave—was at the doors, actually—this terrible storm started. Came down in sheets, you know. And Terry couldn't get a taxi. And if Terry can't get one, nobody can."

"Terry's one of the doormen at the Algonquin, sir," Tony Cook said. "He's very good at getting cabs."

Shapiro said, "Thanks, Cook," keeping it formal for the woman who seemed so easily distracted from her husband's violent death.

"It was quite a storm, Mrs. Claye," he said. "Ought to have cooled things off, but doesn't seem to have much. So you missed the last train, Mrs. Claye? And?"

"Got a room at the hotel, of course. They're usually booked solid, but I was lucky. Of course, they know Roger. He often goes there for lunch. So they went to some trouble for me."

Shapiro said he saw. "Actually, of course, I could have used the suite at the Plaza," Faith Claye said. "But it was still raining, and there still weren't any cabs and the Plaza is farther away than Grand Central, you know."

Shapiro agreed that the Plaza, on Fifty-ninth Street, is

farther from the Algonquin, on Forty-fourth, than the Grand Central Terminal at Forty-second and Lexington is.

Since she was in the city, had she tried to get in touch with her husband?

"I tried to reach him on the phone. Here and at the Plaza. He wasn't either place. I don't know where he was."

They stood up, and Shapiro thanked Mrs. Claye for help and expressed his sympathy and, again, their regret at having had to bother her at such a bad time. She accepted the apology with grace and lowered eyes.

Probably they would have to be in touch with her again, Shapiro told her. Or somebody would. Would she be here, at West Eleventh Street, or did she plan to go back to Bedford Hills?

"Not here," she said. "It's so empty here, without the staff or anything. I think I'll have them come in and get things ready, you know. Yes, that's what I think I'll do. And stay up at the Plaza until I do. Anyway, I'll—I'll have to get some suitable clothes, won't I? And, I suppose people will be calling. And there may be newspaper people. At the Plaza they can—well, arrange things."

Shapiro thought that would be an excellent idea, and that he would tell "them" where she could be reached, if reaching her became necessary.

They left her sitting on the sofa in the empty room of the empty house and walked over to Sixth Avenue.

"Taking it well, isn't she?" Tony said. "After, how many years have they been married, Nate?"

"Quite a while," Shapiro said. "Married in sixty-two, according to *Who's Who*. Yes, she seems to be bearing up very well, Tony."

"Too well?"

"It's hard to tell about things like that," Shapiro said. "People react differently. Because people are different, of course. I think you'd better go up to the Algonquin, don't you? While I go back and fill Bill in."

"Yeah," Cook said. "I'll see what's going on at the Algonquin. What went on last night, anyway. Not much to fill the captain in with, is there?"

"Not yet," Shapiro agreed, and flagged down a taxi. They both got in. Tony dropped Shapiro near the headquarters office of Manhattan South, and the cab went back to Sixth Avenue and uptown to Forty-fourth Street. It was well after eleven when Tony went into the Algonquin lobby. A few people were still having breakfast in the Rose Room—not many. Few of the Algonquin's guests are breakfast eaters; most of those who are use room service.

The doorman he passed going into the hotel was not Terry. Terry would not be on until four, and probably wouldn't remember much anyway. Terry would have been busy at around midnight the night before, particularly since it had been raining around midnight.

The desk clerk was a man Tony did not know. He and Rachel have dinner often at the Algonquin, particularly since Charles French Restaurant, such an easy walk from Gay Street, no longer exists. They have never checked in at the Algonquin. There has always been Rachel's Gay Street apartment; and now there is Tony's, one floor above.

Tony explained who he was and what he wanted. The clerk wasn't sure he ought to. Tony showed the gold shield. The clerk guessed maybe it would be all right. Mrs. Claye? The name sounded familiar, somehow. It would become more familiar, Tony thought. He said, "Yes, Mrs. Roger Claye. She may have registered as Faith Claye, I suppose."

The clerk would look it up. He did look it up, going out of sight to do so. Probably, Tony thought, to get an assistant manager's O.K.

He was more affable when he returned. Yes, Mrs. Roger Claye had checked in at twelve fourteen that morning. They had found her a room, although he gathered it had been difficult. "We're usually booked solid, Mr. Cook. Particularly at this time of year, with people coming back to town." But they had found Mrs. Claye a nice corner room on the fourth floor. She had signed out at a little after nine this morning.

Cook thanked him. "Wasn't it a Roger Claye got killed last night?" the clerk said. "A newspaperman of some kind?" Tony Cook agreed that a man named Roger Claye had been killed the night before and that he had been a newspaperman of some sort, then he said, "By the way, is a man named Brian Mead registered here?"

"Oh, yes, sir. Mr. Mead lives here. Has for more than a year. He has a suite here. The fourth-floor suite. Very famous man, Mr. Mead is. Writes plays, you know. Many of our guests are theater people, you know. It's a tradition, you know."

Tony did know. All three times.

"I wonder," he said, "if Mr. Mead had supper here last night? After the theater?"

"I understand he often does," the clerk said. "I wouldn't really know about last night. I'm on days this week."

"If he did have, he'd probably have signed the check," Tony said. "Since he's a guest here. Could you find out for me?"

Well, the clerk supposed he could. If it was important.

"Just something we'd like to know," Tony told him.

Well, the clerk supposed it would be all right.

He disappeared again and was gone for several minutes. Tony lighted a cigarette and waited. People were drifting into the lobby now, finding seats near small tables. A bell tinkled on one of the tables where two men were sitting. One of the men was trim in a blue suit; the other was notable chiefly for the plenitude of his beard. But they were, evidently, alike in being early drinkers.

The desk clerk returned. Yes, Mr. Mead had signed supper checks the night before. A bar check for three Irish coffees. A restaurant check for a lobster thermidor and one for cold roast beef, garni.

The number of the room assigned Mrs. Claye? Yes, he

knew she had checked out of it. Four twelve? Thank you. And of Mr. Mead's suite? Suite Four A? Thanks again.

He might as well, Tony thought. Sometimes you don't realize there are gaps until you try to fill them in. He found a house phone. He got Suite Four A, which consisted of "Yeah?" All right, sure this was Brian Mead. And who, at such an ungodly hour, was this? Almost noon did not seem so ungodly an hour to Tony Cook, but he did not debate the matter. He was Detective Anthony Cook, New York Police Department, and he would appreciate a few minutes of Mr. Mead's time. Oh, just to check up on a couple of routine matters. Well, connected with the death of one Roger Claye.

What the hell was Brian Mead supposed to know about that? Probably nothing, of course. Entirely routine. Shouldn't take more than ten minutes or so. "Thanks, Mr. Mead. We appreciate it."

Mead was quick to open the door of Suite A on the fourth floor of the Hotel Algonquin. Mead was about five feet eight and probably in his early thirties and wore a pair of shorts. Period. He was broad-shouldered and muscular. He looked, to Tony, more like a welterweight fighter than a playwright.

The suite was of two rooms. The room beyond that into which Mead led Tony Cook had an unmade double bed in it and, next to the bed, a chair with clothing tossed on it. Mead didn't, evidently, care much about preserving the creases in his trousers.

There was a breakfast tray on a table in front of a small sofa in the sitting room of the suite. Mead said, "Well," and went to sit on the sofa and to pour coffee from a silvery pot. Tony said, "Good morning, Mr. Mead. I—"

"Is it?" Mead said. "I wouldn't know. Mornings are lousy, mostly. Get on with it, why don't you? Oh, sit down, if you want to. Hell, if you want to, get a glass out of the bathroom and have some coffee. If there's any left." He swirled the pot and liquid swished in it.

Tony said, "No, thanks."

Mead said, "Okay, get on with it, then."

"Last night," Tony said, "you and Mrs. Roger Claye had dinner here and then went to the theater. That right?"

"Sure. And last night Faith's husband got himself shot to death. So?"

"Early this morning, actually," Tony said. "Down at the Sentinel Building. After he had told his wife he wouldn't make it up to Bedford Hills until today. And Mrs. Claye agreed to come in to town and go to the theater with you. Right so far? And you and Mrs. Claye are good friends, I take it?"

"Not all that good," Mead said, answering, Tony thought, a question which had not been asked. "For the rest, yes. Anyway, she told me Claye had called and said he couldn't make it to the country. Why he couldn't, or said he couldn't, you'll have to ask her."

Tony realized that. He merely wondered if, during the evening, Mrs. Claye had tried to get in touch with her husband. To tell him she was in town, perhaps. Perhaps to suggest he might join them for dinner. Perhaps for the theater?

"While we were having cocktails," Mead said, "she tried to reach him by telephone. What she told me, anyway. Tried the Plaza, where he sometimes stays, and then this house of theirs downtown. No soap either time. What she told me, anyway. When she came back from the phone booth. Wouldn't have asked him to go to the theater, because I only had two seats and she knew it, because I'd told her I'd only got them by a fluke. Sold out into January, *Roundabout* is. And Jimmy Brownley's a lucky bastard, for my money."

"Brownley?"

"Wrote the damn thing. And I do mean the damn thing. Giraffe lost in a traffic circle, for Christ's sake. Not that I'm not all for Jimmy's making a wad. But for this tripe—Jesus!"

"You've had some hits yourself, from what we hear, Mr. Mead."

"Two on now, yeah. *Hayride*'s pretty solid. *Place Your Bets* slowing down a bit. Only, neither of them's about a giraffe. Not that Jimmy isn't a grand guy. Salt of the earth, whatever that's supposed to mean."

"All right. And after the play, you came back here for a nightcap. Before Mrs. Claye went to catch her train. Tried to, anyway. And couldn't get a cab and checked in here instead. While you were having your nightcaps, did Mrs. Claye try again to get in touch with her husband? At the Plaza, or their town house? Or, maybe, his office?"

"After we'd ordered," Mead said, "she said she'd give Roger one more try. Came back and said it was no soap again, either at the hotel or the house. She did say that maybe he'd gone down to the *Sentinel*, but that there was no use trying him there because the switchboard would have closed down for the night, and that if they were plugged through to anyplace it would be to the city desk, and he'd never hear it ring from his office."

"She did think he might have gone down there, though?"

"Said he did now and then. To look things up. Hell, he may have gone to the theater, and gone down to blast somebody else's play."

Tony hadn't gathered that Claye reviewed plays. He said so.

"No. Now and then he goes out of his way to savage one. For what he calls 'almost criminal permissiveness, and dangerous contributions to the breakdown of our social system.' And probably threats to national security and perhaps Communist-inspired. *International* communism, you understand."

Tony said he understood. He said, "It sounds a little as if you were speaking from personal experience, Mr. Mead."

Mead lifted his coffee cup and looked into it. He appeared to find it empty and put it down again. He lighted a cigarette and regarded the lighted end for some seconds. Then he nodded his head.

"All right," he said, "maybe I led with my chin. But you can always look it up, can't you? In the files. All right, pretty much what he said about *Place Your Bets* after it opened last spring. Didn't do it any good, probably. Some right-wing cranks take what he says for gospel. What he says and what the sons of Birchites say. 'Sons of Birchites' is pretty good, don't you think? Wish I'd thought of it first. An editorial writer on some small-town paper in Connecticut came up with it. Paper in Fairfield County, for God's sake. Lost advertisers, probably, for saying it. And proved that not all newspapers are as moribund as the *Sentinel*. Didn't know he was spiting his face, feet of Claye didn't."

Tony Cook raised his eyebrows and shook his head.

"Mrs. Claye was one of the backers of *Place Your Bets*," Mead said. "About a ten percent interest. And is doing damn well out of it, in spite of her husband's blast. Cutting off his nose is what Mr. Claye was doing, and probably didn't know it."

"Didn't know his wife had invested in this play of yours, you mean?"

"Maybe didn't. Anyway, it's her money, all the millions of it. What Claye made—whatever it was—was just petty cash to Faith."

"She often back plays, do you know?"

"I don't know about often. Money in *Place Your Bets* and in a new one of mine that's coming in in November, if it doesn't fall apart." He drew deeply on his cigarette. "As it probably will," he said.

He lifted his coffee cup again. It was still empty.

5

NOT MUCH from that, Tony thought, riding down from the fourth floor to the Algonquin's lobby. Mrs. Claye had thought, or implied she thought, her husband went more frequently to his office at the *Sentinel* than others thought he had. Since offices at the *Sentinel* were presumably empty in the middle of the night, there would be few, if any, there to check on Roger Claye's nocturnal use of his office. So Mrs. Claye might know best. Which didn't narrow things down; which opened them up.

Faith Claye's room at the hotel the night before had been on the same floor as Brian Mead's suite. Probably coincidence; obviously convenient, if convenience was wanted. Mead had been quick to deny any close friendship with Faith Claye; had answered a question not asked. So? Claye had written derogatory things about one of Mead's plays, but apparently without interfering too much with its success. So?

The Algonquin's pleasant lounge was almost full, although it was only a few minutes after noon. Drinks were being served at the small tables. Two long-haired young men were at the table Rachel and Tony tried to get when they came early for dinner, as they sometimes did.

The Oak Room was almost empty. In an hour it would be jammed. I ought to go downtown, Tony thought. Nate will, about now, be showing up at the lunch joint. Get a hamburger and a beer and, if Nate's there, fill him in. Cheaper by a lot than eating here. Still, I like it here. Even alone, I like it here. Tony went into the Oak Room. There was no problem about a table for one.

It was almost two thirty when Tony Cook climbed the stairs to the squad room of Homicide, Manhattan South. Lieutenant Shapiro was in the captain's office. Tony went into Shapiro's office and waited. He waited half an hour before Nathan Shapiro came in. Shapiro's long face was mournful. Of course, it almost always was. It cheered, just perceptibly, when he was onto something. It was clear that now he wasn't; clear even before he shook his head. He sat down at his desk, which had papers on it.

What Tony had to tell him didn't cheer him greatly. Tony hadn't supposed it would. It was interesting that Faith Claye and Brian Mead had had rooms on the same floor at the Algonquin, and that Mead had, unasked, disclaimed anything but the most casual friendship with his dinner and theater companion of the night before. Did Tony think—?

Tony had only a shrug to answer that. Mmm. Might be worth looking into further, of course. And that, in New York, Mrs. Claye had tried to get in touch with her husband. Yes, possibly to be sure he was tucked away safely for the night. Just as possibly to tell him she was in town and to arrange for them to meet after the theater.

As for Shapiro himself—he gestured toward the papers on the desk in front of him.

Roger Claye had been a male Caucasian, five feet ten

inches tall; weighing about a hundred and sixty pounds. He had been somewhere in his fifties, and well nourished. He had had no major physical ailments. He had a slug from a .25 revolver in his brain. Death had been almost instantaneous. He had eaten about six hours before he died. He had had two or three drinks before dinner; probably no alcohol after it.

The precinct boys had been busy, as behooved them. So had the lab boys.

Claye had not, apparently, been working at his typewriter when he was shot. There had been no paper in his typewriter and no discarded sheets in his wastebasket. If he had been looking something up in the newspaper morgue, he had not made notes on his memo pad. It was on the desk in front of him, with a pencil beside it. Nothing had been written on the top sheet; there were no indentations on it to suggest that the top sheet had, in fact, been a second sheet, with the actual top sheet torn away.

There were fingerprints on the desk top and on the drawer pulls. All but two or three were Claye's own. On the chair which faced the desk—the visitor's chair—there were further prints of Claye's and a few smudges which were not going to do anybody any good.

The slug extracted from his brain was distorted from its contact with his skull. It might provide comparison identification when they found something to compare it with. The identification would be susceptible to challenge by a defense attorney if they managed to come up with a defendant.

Shapiro's tone did not suggest much optimism about that.

The precinct detectives had come up with odds and ends of information.

Leroy Sampson, managing editor of the *Sentinel,* was a native of Alabama and a graduate of Tuscaloosa. He had got his B.A. there, had played first base on the baseball team and had had a tryout with minor-league professionals. Either he had changed his mind about a career as a professional athlete or it had been changed for him after the tryout. He had had his first newspaper job on a paper in Montgomery. He had later worked on a paper in Athens, Georgia. He had then worked, for upwards of three years, on an Atlanta paper. He had been in New York for a little more than fifteen years. He had been an assistant city editor on the morning *Sentinel* and, after it was sold, on the evening edition. He had been city editor of the *Sentinel*, after it became only an afternoon newspaper, for about a year and had then been promoted to managing editor.

He had never, it appeared, been too well liked by staff members of the paper. He was, evidently, a martinet. One reporter, who didn't want to be quoted by name, had referred to Sampson as a "goddamn top sergeant."

Sampson was married and had an apartment on Park Avenue.

Jason Wainwright, editor, was a childless widower. He lived at the Fifth Avenue Hotel at Fifth Avenue and Ninth Street. He was in his late seventies and the *Sentinel*'s oldest living employee, having been on it, in increasingly important capacities, when it had been owned by Lester Mason and had been in its palmiest days. Wainwright was not listed in *Who's Who in America*. He was a member of The Players and, according to the clubhouse manager, lunched there regularly on Saturdays.

Russel Perryman was prominently in *Who's Who*. Born in Boston, September 30, 1909; son of James and Mary Cabot Perryman; educated at Kent and Harvard; inherited a small chain of grocery stores and expanded it into the Perry Stores.

Tony said "Wow!" when he read that, with Nathan Shapiro regarding him sadly across the desk. "Damn near as big as the A and P, isn't it?"

Shapiro nodded his head.

Perryman had married Ruth Foxwood in 1934. Ruth was deceased, no date of her decease given in the biography. A son, David, had been born in 1949. When, Tony thought, his father was forty. Russel and Ruth Perryman had taken their time about it.

Perryman had described himself as "merchant and publisher." He was a member of the Harvard Club and of the Union League Club. "Home" was an address on Sutton Place, New York City.

"One of those big town houses," Shapiro said, and added, "His son doesn't live there. Has an apartment down in your part of town. Grove Street."

Tony Cook's part of town is Greenwich Village. He recently moved from West Twelfth Street to Gay Street, the apartment a floor above Rachel Farmer's having become vacant. Gay Street is not noticeably more convenient to squad headquarters in the East Twenties than Twelfth Street was, but to Tony it is a good deal more convenient.

Tony said he knew where Grove Street was.

"Young Perryman works on his father's newspaper," Shapiro said. "On the city staff, whatever that is." His tone indicated that he mentioned an insoluble mystery.

"The room we were in first this morning," Tony said. "The city room. City staff works there. Handles the local news. Writes it. Copyreads it and writes headlines on it. And sends it along to the composing room." He thought of adding, "As you know perfectly well, Nate," and decided not to.

Nathan Shapiro said he saw, but spoke as if he didn't.

He's been talking to the captain, Tony thought. Saying "Ouch!" Saying, "Not another one, Bill? Not over my head again!" And meaning it. Anyway, thinking he means it.

"Works the eight-to-four shift," Shapiro said. "The *Sentinel* has five editions a day. Used to be six, the precinct boys say. The Home Edition, the Night Edition—which comes out on the street a little before two—and the Complete Final, with Wall Street Closings. And then two more Complete Finals, the last containing Complete Sports. There used to be four complete finals, they say. They dropped the last one a couple of years ago."

"Probably because they play big-league games mostly at night, now," Tony said.

"Could be," Shapiro said. "And one of the other reporters told a precinct man that David Perryman is known as 'the office pink.'"

Tony said, "Huh?"

"I don't know," Shapiro said. "Possibly caught voting Democratic once. From what I gather, 'pink' would cover a good many shades of color on the *Sentinel.*"

"Anything lighter than coal black," Tony said. "If Claye's columns were characteristic, and I guess they were."

"Probably," Shapiro said. "It's supported Reagan for years, according to Bill Weigand. Thinks Ford too liberal. Bill says Dorian reads it sometimes. To keep from getting low blood pressure, was the way he put it."

"She sounds like Rachel," Tony said.

"Possibly a little," Nathan agreed. "Except Mrs. Weigand has green eyes. Speaking of black. And going back to Sampson for a moment. Until three-four years ago, no black person—I mean Negro—ever was a 'Mr.' or a 'Mrs.' on the *Sentinel.* Just—oh, 'Jones' for the man. 'The Jones woman' for the female. By order of Leroy Sampson, managing editor."

Tony said, "Mmm," and added, "Well, he's from Alabama, after all."

Shapiro agreed that was that. "And this isn't getting us much of anywhere, is it? Some Communist killed Claye, the way Mr. Perryman seems to think? Or maybe Mrs. Claye's boyfriend, if any? And how much weight can Perryman throw around with the commissioner?"

"Not too much, probably," Tony said. "Wrong party. Still—"

"Yes," Shapiro said. "And we're supposed to come up with some left-wing terrorist, member of what they call a revolutionary army."

"Make everybody happy," Tony said.

Shapiro shook his head. "Not us," he said. "What we

want is a killer. Somebody who sat across a desk from Claye and shot him with a twenty-five revolver. Let's think about the physical layout for a while, Tony."

Precinct detectives had come through with a memo on the physical layout of the Sentinel Building. The building was six stories. Space was rented on the ground floor to a pharmacy, which was as much snack bar as drugstore. "Seems most of the *Sentinel* people take their coffee break there after the first edition goes to press." The pharmacy had entrances both from the street and from the lobby. So did a liquor store next to it. The *Sentinel*'s business office occupied about half the ground floor.

There were two elevators, both push-button-operated. "Had operators until about five years ago. Had a starter nine to five."

At either end of the lobby there was a staircase. "Everybody working on the second floor is supposed to walk up."

"Save wear and tear on the elevators?" Tony suggested.

Shapiro smiled faintly and said, "Possibly."

The second-floor workers who were supposed to plod upstairs were members of the editorial staff—city-room reporters and copyreaders, and editorial writers under Jason Wainwright. Simms and three other men were under Wainwright. The three other editorial writers had offices on the Broadway side of the building. Their offices were like the one Claye had been killed in. All the offices on that side of the second floor had been empty when Claye was shot. The city room had been deserted until the lobster trick came on.

The composing room occupied the other part of the second floor, across the main corridor where the elevators were. And also the stairway to be walked up. Shapiro put a just discernible question mark after "composing room."

"Where they set type," Tony told him. "Put the paper together, physically. Ready for the presses, which would be in the basement. Where we heard them start rolling."

Shapiro said, "I see, Tony," in a not-happy voice. He

added, "I suppose they walk up, too? The people who set type?"

"Composing room people," Tony said. "I suppose they must."

The sports and financial departments were on the third floor. Those who worked there were permitted to use the elevators, although the sportswriters and editors were encouraged to walk up. The photographers were also quartered on the third floor, in the rear. There may have been sportswriters and an assistant editor on that floor as late as midnight, handling copy on night ball games. Precinct was working on that.

The advertising department occupied the fourth floor. The advertising manager, whose name was Burton Evans, had a corner office and his assistant a smaller one, adjacent. Half a dozen advertising salesmen had desks. Evans, queried by precinct detectives, was sure nobody in his department had been in the office the previous night. "Why should anybody be? We're nine to five."

The fifth floor was occupied by the Consolidated Features Service, the syndicate which distributed, among other features, the Roger Claye columns. It was only partially owned by the *Sentinel* and distributed other columns, ranging from those advising troubled readers on matrimonial and related subjects to book reviews. It also, during the season, sent out a weekly theater roundup written by the *Sentinel*'s drama critic. It syndicated a movie-review column by its own movie reviewer, one Elinor Gibson.

"Rachel knows her, I think. Wades around in artistic values, Rachel says. Very long and pretty confusing pieces, Rachel says."

Shapiro said, "Mmm." He is not greatly interested in the art of the cinema, although he and Rose sometimes go to movies.

Shapiro looked at his watch, which showed him three thirty-five. And nothing done. Time frittered away.

The sixth—and top—floor of the Sentinel Building was the realm of Russel Perryman, owner and publisher. He was not in his office when precinct detectives went to see him. His secretary was at her desk. Mr. Perryman had gone uptown to the Perry Stores Building, as he did most mornings. He would be back after lunch. Probably, although with this tragic thing he might, of course, alter his routine.

If they wanted to talk to Mr. Johnson, it probably could be arranged. Mr. Johnson? "He's head of our legal department. Perhaps he can help you."

The two precinct detectives rather doubted it.

"Or perhaps Mr. Dickson? I'm sure Mr. Perryman will want to cooperate any way he can."

"Mr. Dickson?"

"A vice-president of Perry Stores. He has an office down here. So he and Mr. Perryman can consult when they need to."

The detectives had decided they wouldn't need to bother Mr. Dickson, an executive of a grocery chain seeming at some remove from a newspaper columnist.

"And that's the setup," Shapiro said. "For what good it does us. Anybody could have walked into the building and gone up a flight of stairs and shot Claye in his office, with damn little risk of being seen."

"Anybody," Tony said, "who knew he was going to be in his office."

"Or followed him to his office from wherever he'd been. And we don't know where that was, do we? Not at the Eleventh Street house, apparently, if his wife is right. Not in the suite at the Plaza, again on her say-so. And, of course, if a Plaza desk clerk told her the truth."

"All evening at the *Sentinel* office waiting for a murderer to show up?"

"Or working on his column," Shapiro said. "Only there doesn't seem to be any column, does there? Unless whoever killed him took it along. Which, far's we know, might have been the whole idea. To see that that particular column wasn't printed."

"Why, Nate?"

Nathan Shapiro hadn't the faintest idea. He spoke as one who feels he never will have.

"The thing is," he said, "we're just groping around in the dark. We know where he was born and that he married twice and wrote a syndicated column which raised Dorian Weigand's blood pressure. And your Rachel's blood pressure."

"And that he's dead and was a member of the John Birch Society."

"But nothing about *him,* Tony. A name and a few scattered facts. Not who he *was*. Named and fingerprinted, and we can get his Social Security number and find out how much he made a year. All *what* he was. Not *who* he was. Did he wake up bright-eyed in the morning? Did he like a hearty breakfast? Did he like night spots, or did he go to bed early? All the little things which make somebody a person, instead of a name. Because it was a person who got killed, wasn't it?"

"It could have been an institution, Nate. That got killed, I mean. Could be a column got killed. The man—well, the man almost incidentally."

Shapiro said, "Mmm." He added, "I suppose so. More or less what Perryman thinks, isn't it? But I don't know, Tony. All pretty pat, somehow. However—"

He looked at his watch. It was almost four o'clock. He and Tony Cook were working the eight-to-four shift. Theoretically, as always.

"Maybe we can get a little more out of Mrs. Claye," Shapiro said. "Find out, maybe, what made him tick. Maybe she'll be at the Plaza."

He got an outside line and dialed the Plaza Hotel. He got the desk.

Yes, Mrs. Claye had picked up the key to the Clayes' leased suite. But she had left word—very firm word—that she did not want to be disturbed.

"This is a police call," Shapiro said. "I'm a police lieutenant. So please put me through to her." He listened a moment. "Yes," he said. "I realize that the Clayes are rather special guests, and that her father was for years and that you don't want to do anything that would disturb her at a time like this. Suppose you ring the suite and ask her if I can see her for a few minutes? Shapiro. Lieutenant Nathan Shapiro. One of the officers who talked to her earlier today."

The clerk said, well, he guessed he could do that.

Shapiro waited. He waited what seemed like a long time. Finally—

"Mrs. Claye's suite doesn't answer, sir. Probably she has gone out."

Or, of course, wasn't answering her phone. No, they needn't bother to page Mrs. Claye. He would try again later, or perhaps in the morning.

"This guy Simms?" Tony said. "The associate editor down at the *Sentinel*? The one who was writing the editorial about Claye?"

Shapiro hadn't got the idea that Simms knew Claye very well. Still, he might be a place to grope.

"I'll stop by and see him," Shapiro said. "More or less on my way home. We'll pick it up again in the morning. Meet you—let's say at the Sentinel Building. Nose around a little there. Maybe have a little talk with Mr. Perryman himself, if he's not too occupied with groceries."

Tony Cook said, "O.K.," and stood up. He had turned toward the door of Shapiro's small office when Shapiro spoke again.

"This Grove Street," Shapiro said. "Not too far from where you live now, is it?"

"Only a few blocks," Cook said. "Young Perryman?"

"If he happens to be home," Shapiro said. "Supposed to be off work at four. Ought to be getting home about now."

"Find out how pink he is?"

"We could stand to know," Shapiro said. "His father

and Mrs. Claye's father were business associates. And it could be Bradford got his son-in-law the job on the paper, couldn't it? And David Perryman is—well, part of the family. Whatever he can tell us, Tony. About anything, I guess."

Tony said "O.K." again, and this time walked out of Shapiro's office. The four-to-midnight shift was occupying desks in the squad room. Detective (1st gr.) Cunningham was on a telephone, listening to the shift's first squeal.

Tony went downstairs. It was still hot on the street. The freshening breezes of autumn ought to be along any day now. Or any week. Not yet, obviously.

It was ten after four. If David Perryman left the Sentinel Building at four, he could hardly reach his apartment on Grove Street before around four thirty. Assuming he went directly home; did not stop somewhere for a beer. It was a good afternoon for a beer, perhaps in some air-conditioned bar. Tony Cook started to walk crosstown toward Gay Street.

Perhaps it would make sense to buy a small car of his own. A little Volks, maybe. There was a garage on Christopher Street where he could park it. They'd nick him, of course. So would payments on even the smallest Volks. But so would taxicabs. Life had been simpler when Homicide South was in the West Twenties instead of on the east side of town.

Tony walked west.

6

Shapiro went down to Canal Street by subway. The local train wasn't crowded. It was merely hot and stuffy. There were two *Sentinel* trucks on the cross street south of the Sentinel Building. Waiting, presumably, for bundles of newspapers of a late edition.

Shapiro climbed the stairs to the second floor. The arrow on the "Enquiries" sign at the head of the stairs pointed up the corridor. But the double doorway opening into what Nathan now knew to be the city room stood open, and he went that way.

There were fewer people in the city room than there had been in the morning, and few of them seemed to be doing much of anything. One man was typing; another was on a telephone. Only one of the three desks which made up the "city desk" was occupied, and the man at it was reading a newspaper. Sampson was not at the set-apart desk under a window in the corner of the big room.

The *Sentinel* obviously was simmering down for the day. Probably Peter Simms, associate editor, had folded his typewriter and stolen away. I could have called ahead, Nathan thought. Well, I didn't. He went through the corridor which connected the two halves of the Broadway side of the second floor. The tickers were still chattering in their small, noisy room.

Along the wider hallway, none of the offices on the Broadway side seemed to be occupied. Most of the doors stood open. It must have been rather like this at around midnight, or perhaps at one o'clock that morning.

But at the end of the hallway, the door of Peter Simms's office was closed. Shapiro knocked on it and got a response. The response was "Yes?" which Shapiro accepted as an invitation to open the door.

Simms, at his desk, put down the paper he had been reading. He said, "Afternoon, Lieutenant. Still here? Got it wrapped up?"

"Back here," Shapiro said. "And no, nothing's wrapped up. Maybe you can help us, Mr. Simms."

"Glad to," Simms said. "How?"

"Mr. Claye called his wife about five o'clock last evening," Shapiro said. "He was shot to death here sometime early this morning. We'd like to know what he was doing during those eight or nine hours. Who he was with. What was keeping him here in town."

"Can't help you, I'm afraid. He sure as hell wasn't with me, if that's what you're getting at."

Shapiro assured Simms that that was not what he was getting at and Simms said, "Well?"

Shapiro sat in a chair across the desk from Peter Simms.

"We try to find out all we can in a case like this about the person who was killed," he said. "What his habits were. Who his friends were. What kind of man he was, if you see what I mean. Sometimes that helps to tell us why he was killed. And the why may lead to the who. How well did you know Mr. Claye, Mr. Simms?"

"To say hello to is about all. When we happened to meet, which wasn't often. As I told you, he didn't come to the office much. Sent his copy in. Never talked to him—really talked to him. Said it was a pretty day out. Or a lousy day. Few times I ran into him in the hall."

"So you don't know anything about his personal life?"

"Not a damn thing. For all I know, he was a bluebeard, with closets stuffed with corpses. Or a saint, about to ascend. We—let's say we didn't move in the same circles."

"Can you suggest anybody who did, Mr. Simms? Move in the same circles? Would know whether he was a bluebeard or a saint?"

"No. Oh, I put it extravagantly, of course. Don't suppose he was either. No. I don't know offhand anybody who can tell you much about his personal life. What he thought, what his prejudices were—all that's clear enough from his columns. Our morgue will have a file of them, of course. You can always read up on them, Shapiro."

"We'll probably have to," Shapiro said, and his voice was disgruntled. The half smile appeared on Simms's lips and he nodded his head.

"Any chance, you think, that Mr. Wainwright knew him better?"

"One in a million, at a guess. Wainwright had to read his columns, of course. Part of the job. Read them in proof. Not to approve them in advance. I doubt if they had much other contact. But you can ask Jase, of course. Only it will have to be tomorrow, unless you want to look Jase up at his hotel. He's gone for the day. Tomorrow's page all set up. So, being a sensible man, he's gone home. Which I'm about ready to do, Lieutenant. Unless?"

"I won't keep you," Shapiro said. "Since you didn't really know Mr. Claye and can't think of anybody who might."

"Afraid that's the way it is," Simms said. "Unless—" He paused and looked at the opposite wall for a moment. "You could beard the lion, I suppose," he said. "In his den on the sixth floor. Probably just growl at you. Great man for growling, the owner and publisher is. But he did, I guess, know Claye better than anyone else around here. After all, he hired him. Possibly at Mrs. Claye's suggestion. She was a Bradford, after all. And her father and Perryman were probably buddies. Could be, our owner and publisher was on friendly terms with the Clayes. Sort of all family together, it could have been. But I don't know. Just guessing."

Shapiro said he saw. He said he might have a word with Mr. Perryman, as long as he was there. And assuming Mr. Perryman, also, had not gone for the day.

Simms merely shrugged at that. As Shapiro left the associate editor's small office, Simms stood up behind his desk. He said, "Don't let him bite you, Lieutenant."

Shapiro made what could have been an appreciative laughing sound. He did not go back along the hall to the city room, but instead took the short corridor to his right that led him past Wainwright's door and into the main corridor. He walked down that to the elevators. He might as well, he thought, take a chance of being growled at. Or perhaps bitten. Simms apparently did not hold his employer in high regard. There had, however, seemed to be affection in his voice when he spoke of his immediate superior, Jason Wainwright. It could be that all was not serene in the staff of the New York *Sentinel.* On the other hand, of course, newspaper people were a sort about whom Shapiro knew nothing. They could not be evaluated by so complete an outsider.

From the indicator, one of the two elevators was going up. It went from the third floor to the fourth as Shapiro watched. The other elevator was at the sixth floor and appeared to be sitting there. Shapiro pressed the down button. The sixth-floor light went out, and the car started down. It reached the third floor—sports and financial departments, Shapiro remembered—and stopped there. Shapiro again pressed the down button.

The elevator obeyed. It reached the second floor and opened its door.

Nathan Shapiro started to step inside. And stopped. The car's light was off. It was dim inside. But light enough to see by.

The man lying on the floor of the car was a tall man. He lay facedown. There was blood on the floor and the man was still bleeding. From, Shapiro thought, a wound in the upper chest. Blood was bubbling out of the man.

The elevator door started to close. Shapiro reached in and the door came against his arm and opened again. Shapiro flicked the light switch on the panel; the light came on. He pushed the red EMERG STOP button, which would hold the door open, and went into the car. He crouched by the bleeding man. The man was still alive. But he wouldn't, Shapiro thought, be alive long. Not at the rate he was losing blood.

It was then ten minutes of five.

* * * * *

Tony Cook did not hurry on his way west, crosstown with the sun in his face. Even walking in the shade on the south side of the street, it was hot. When, on Sixth Avenue, he turned south, there was almost no shade at all, even on the west side of the avenue. Between Ninth and Tenth Streets, Tony stopped at Hugo's for a beer.

Charles French Restaurant had once had Michelob on draught, but Charles had gone, and draught beer with it. At Hugo's bar, which was hardly any cooler than the street, Tony settled for Budweiser from a bottle. He lingered over it. Probably David Perryman would stop for a beer himself on his way from the *Sentinel* office to Grove Street.

It was almost half-past five when Tony Cook found the Grove Street address. It was half a block from Sheridan Square, which is by no means square. It was a three-story "brownstone"—made of brick. Tony climbed the five steps and went into the entry hall.

There were only three mailboxes on the wall in the small lobby—one, evidently, for each floor. David Perryman lived, from the arrangement of the mailboxes, on the second floor. Tony pressed Perryman's bell and waited to be clicked in. Or, if young Perryman was the cautious sort, to be gratingly asked for identification.

Neither of these things happened. A second pressure, more sustained this time, resulted again in nothing. Probably, Perryman had had more than one beer on his way home. Or was not coming home at all. This was Friday—and a damned long Friday. On Friday afternoons, those who can often leave early for Long Island or Westchester. Or, conceivably, for rural New Jersey.

As the son of the owner of the *Sentinel*—and of a supermarket chain—David Perryman was presumably one of those who could leave early. Perhaps Saturday was a day off for him from the *Sentinel* city desk.

I could go home and shower, Tony thought. Get the air conditioning going. Wait until time to go down a flight of stairs and knock on Rachel's door. Two quick ones, a pause, and then a third. So she'll know who it is.

Well, wait another few minutes and then call it a day? Too bad there isn't anything to sit on. Wait until, say, a quarter of six.

At a quarter of six, Tony pressed the doorbell button once more. Young Perryman might have been in the shower, with water running noisily. There was still no response. The hell with it. David Perryman could be seen at any time; asked at any time whether he had known Roger Claye. Probably he hadn't. If Claye had been a visitor at the elder Perryman's house, it probably was after David had left the house in Sutton Place for his own apartment in Grove Street; presumably for his own life there.

Tony opened the door to the street. He was confronted

by a tall young man in a summer jacket and darker summer slacks. He had reddish-brown hair and a rather long, noticeably mobile face. It was his height as much as anything else that made Tony take a chance. Like father, like son, perhaps.

"You wouldn't be Mr. Perryman, would you?" Tony said, backing into it.

"No reason why not," the tall youngish man said. "You looking for me?"

Tony explained who he was and that he'd like a few minutes of Mr. Perryman's time.

"About Claye's death, I suppose," Perryman said. "Don't know how I can help you, but sure, come on up if you want to."

Tony did want to, if only mildly. He followed Perryman, after Perryman had used his door key, up a flight of carpeted stairs to where Perryman used his key on another door.

The apartment was typical of those in converted town houses. It had two large rooms, connected by a narrow hallway with a bath opening off it. There would be a smaller room opening off each of the large ones. One of the small rooms would face the street; the other, probably used as a kitchen, would have a window in the rear, overlooking the backyard. Or, if it went to that, the garden.

"Sit down somewhere," Perryman said. "I'm going to have a beer. Want one? Or I can get you something else. Martini, if you'd rather. Or don't you drink on duty? Or with people you're supposed to question?"

Tony said he'd be glad to have a beer. He added that it was a good day for cold beer. Perryman said it sure was and that he'd get the air conditioning going. He flicked a switch on his way to the kitchen, which was where Tony had assumed it would be.

There were plenty of places to sit in the big living room. Money had been spent on the room, and spent with taste. Possibly, of course, an interior decorator's taste. Tony did not know how well newspaper reporters were paid nowadays. When he had, briefly, been a copyboy, reporters had grumbled about their wages. But that had been a long time ago, probably before the Newspaper Guild. Which had made newspaper publishers grumble. Of course, David Perryman's father was a millionaire. Probably several times a millionaire. Which would help.

Perryman came back into the room, carrying two opened bottles and two glasses. By their special shape, they were bottles of Michelob. Perryman sat down in a deep chair near the one Tony had chosen. He put a bottle of Michelob and a glass on the small table in front of it and reached the other glass and bottle across to a table near Tony Cook's chair. He leaned forward a little in his own.

He said, "Well, what do you want to know? Where was I at midnight last night?"

"Not especially," Tony told him, and poured beer into his glass. The glass, like the beer, had been chilled. "Unless you were down at the *Sentinel* office. We've no reason to think you were."

"I was here," David Perryman said. "Here and in bed and probably—by then—asleep. We weren't much keeping track of time." He poured beer into his own glass, carefully not heading it up. "The rest of the 'we' was female," Perryman said. "In case you're wondering."

"I wasn't," Tony said. "But I assume this girl can confirm you were in bed with her last night. If it came to a point where we needed confirmation. Which I've no reason to think it will."

"Sure she will," Perryman said. "No secret about it. You want her name and address?"

"No," Tony said. "Not now, Mr. Perryman. And you can take the chip off your shoulder, if you'd just as soon. We don't think you killed Claye. Why would you?"

Perryman drank beer. He said, "No reason. He was an all-right guy. As reactionary sons of bitches go. I had nothing against him, as *him*. I'm not partial to his tribe. Maybe you've gathered that. Down at the office. Maybe Boss Sampson's told you I'm a Communist. Boring from within. Maybe that's why you're here, huh?"

"No," Tony said. "Nobody's called you a Communist, Mr. Perryman. Are you, by the way?"

"Hell, no. They're worse off than we are, I guess. At least we can say, 'Ouch, that hurts,' out loud without being put in loony bins."

It had been a long time since Tony had heard that expression. Perhaps youth was retrogressing. Certainly, he and Perryman were on a diverging course from the one he had planned.

"What I wanted to talk to you about," Tony said, "was Mr. Claye. What kind of a man he was. Apart from his political views. You knew him, probably."

"A little," Perryman said. "He was around the house a few times while I was still living at home. He married the daughter of an old friend of Dad's, and they came around now and then. A while back. When I was just a kid, actually. When he first started writing that column of his. You've read that column? Dad thinks it's gospel."

Tony shook his head.

"It's a real stinker. Of course, you could say that about Dad's whole paper. It's more a house organ for the reactionaries, actually. Like the *Daily Worker* was for the Communist Party. You know what? We even edited AP copy to cut out any reaction to the statements of men like Reagan. Not supposed to. Violation of our franchise, actually. Supposed to edit only for length, you know."

Tony didn't know. He did know that they kept wandering from the subject, which was the personality of the late Roger Claye.

"About Claye," Tony said. "You did know him at one time? When you were, as you say, a kid?"

"The way a kid knows an old man," Perryman said. "Which isn't very well, I suppose."

"He was in his fifties," Tony said. "What it says in *Who's Who,* anyway. Not an antique, exactly."

"When I was around fifteen," Perryman said, "he seemed like an old man to me. Oh, all right. One's point of view changes. But I remember feeling his wife was more my age. More my generation, that is. Of course, that isn't really true. She's in her thirties somewhere. But a hell of a lot younger than Mr. Claye was."

"But you say that Claye was an all-right guy, Mr. Perryman. Aside from his political views, that is. Pretty much the views your father has, I take it."

"Why Dad hired him," David Perryman said. "Yes, when I was around fifteen-sixteen, he seemed an all-right person. As stuffy old codgers go. But you can't really separate what a man thinks from what he is, can you? What a man thinks *is* what he is."

Tony had reservations to that generalization. He has known reasonably pleasant persons with outlandish ideas. He did not voice his reservations. He said, "I guess so. You saw Mr. Claye and his wife together, I suppose. They seem to be getting along all right?"

"I keep telling you it was when I was just a kid, living at home," Perryman said. "What do kids know about things like that? Far's I know, they got along all right. Didn't throw plates at each other. Dad wouldn't have approved of that. Of course, Faith's twenty years younger than Claye was. More than twenty, from the way they both looked."

"Young enough to be interested in, maybe even looking for, a younger man?"

David emptied his beer glass and, for a moment, regarded it. Then he shook his head.

"I guess it's no comment on that one," he said. "She didn't confide in me. Didn't make passes at me, either. Want another beer? I've got a date in an hour or so."

Tony did not want another beer. He would try not to keep David Perryman from his date. (Or me from mine, he thought.)

"Aside from his ideas you object to," he said, "Claye seemed a pleasant enough man, I take it. Older, of course. But—well, a man who might still be getting around. Might, say, have had a dinner date last night? And perhaps for the whole evening? Until he went down to the Sentinel Building?"

"You mean with a girl? A woman? How would I know?"

"You wouldn't. But you did know him. So you've more to guess on than we have."

"Hell, I wasn't interested in his sex life. Got enough to think about with my own. Seems damn important to kids the age I was then. And we'd assume men Claye's age have—well, lost interest. I realize, now, that he may not have. But, listen, man, I hardly knew him. My old man and the Clayes would be having cocktails. Sometimes I'd have a Coke or something and then get out. The way Dad wanted it. The way I did too."

"Yes," Tony said, "older people can be boring. I remember that much."

"Times I met them were mostly in the summer," Perryman said. "Falls and winters I was in prep school. Where Dad went. Kent. Kent and then Harvard. Business school at Harvard. I just managed to scrape through. Had my way, I'd have gone to Columbia. School of Journalism. But Dad had his way. He usually does."

Tony said, "Mmm." Having met Russel Perryman once, and briefly, he didn't doubt Perryman usually had his way. "This idea you're a radical," Tony said, "a leftist. Any idea how it got started, Mr. Perryman?"

David Perryman grinned at that.

"Could be," he said, "I shot my mouth off a few times. Could be I still do. Also, it probably got around I'm a member of Common Cause. The American Civil Liberties Union, even. Enough, down at the office, to make me a liberal. What they call a 'so-called' liberal. Way Boss Sampson looks at things, that makes me a commie. Way Dad looks at things too, I guess. The Reverend Martin Luther King was a flaming revolutionary, way they look at it. As well as being a nigger, way Sampson looks at it. And—"

The telephone rang, interrupting him. He said, "Sorry. Probably that crazy girl," and went into the narrow corridor to answer the telephone.

Tony finished what little remained of his beer. He listened.

"Yeah, this is David Perryman," he heard, and then, *"What!"* There was a longer pause, then, "Saint Vincent's? Sure I will." There was a briefer pause. "Yes, he is. Sure, I'll tell him."

David Perryman came back into the living room. His face had changed. It had had a cheerful expression up to then. Now it didn't.

"My father's been shot," he said. "Down at the office. They don't know how bad it is, yet. He's at Saint Vincent's. In surgery, they say. I'm going over there and—and wait, I suppose. And if you happened to be here, I was to tell you. And that a Lieutenant Something-or-other was down there. At the office, that is."

"Shapiro," Tony said. "Get along to the hospital. Probably you will have to wait. I'm sorry, Mr. Perryman."

David Perryman was putting on the jacket he had taken off as he had sat down to his beer when Tony Cook went out of the apartment. He was lucky in getting a cab on Seventh Avenue. And, lucky too, of course, that Seventh is one way downtown.

7

Again there were police patrol cars against the curb in front of the Sentinel Building. Again the detective squad was there. It wouldn't be Captain Callahan this time. Callahan worked the eight-to-four. Callahan would be home, or on his way there.

There were two uniformed patrolmen in front of the elevators. Tony Cook showed his badge. "Up on the sixth floor is where they are," the patrolman told him. "Only one of the elevators is working. They're holding the other one up at the sixth."

Tony waited for the working elevator to come down. Nobody got out of it. He got in and pressed the button numbered 6. The car didn't stop on the way up.

There were a good many men on the sixth floor when Cook got out of the elevator. There was one uniformed man. The rest were in civilian clothes and had their gold shields pinned to their jackets. Tony pinned his own on and looked for Nathan Shapiro. After a minute or two, Shapiro came out of Perryman's office. He said, "Hi," and pointed to the other elevator, which had its door open. A photographer was leaning into the car and taking a picture of its inside. He moved away, and Tony looked in.

There was blood on the floor. A good deal of it. He looked at Shapiro. There was blood on both knees of Shapiro's trousers. There was a dab of it on the skirt of his jacket. The blood on the elevator floor was dry, now. So was that on Shapiro's clothes.

"Still in surgery, last we heard," Shapiro said. "So, apparently, still alive. Must have missed the aorta, or just grazed it. Come in here a minute and I'll fill you in."

He led the way into a small office which adjoined Perryman's large corner one. Shapiro sat on a typist's chair behind a desk, and Tony took the other chair in the small room.

"Way it was," Shapiro said, "I was going up to see him. On the chance he knew Claye better than anyone else around here seems to have. When the elevator came down, he was in it. Flat on the floor and bleeding—well, I guess some people would say, like a stuck pig."

The Police Academy teaches New York policemen the rudiments of first aid. Nathan Shapiro had more than the rudiments. What he did not have was any equipment. Neither did anybody in the second-floor city room, to which Shapiro ran for help and a telephone. He did get a couple of towels from desk drawers, and he got the police communications center. In about fifteen minutes, which was good time, considering, he got an ambulance from St. Vincent's. He had turned the prostrate man faceup, by then, and was applying pressure to the hole in the right side of his chest. When he could see the face, he saw that the injured man was Russel Perryman, owner and publisher.

"The top light was off," Shapiro told Cook. "Hadn't just

burned out, as I thought it might have. Been turned off. Made sense to turn it off, of course."

Tony merely waited.

"When I got up here," Shapiro said, "there were half a dozen women weaving around. Looking at the elevators and—well, sort of chirping. Everybody who has an office here has a secretary, of course. The guy from the supermarket chain, the company lawyer, God knows who-all. All the executives, apparently, had gone for the day. Around five, it was by then. Maybe a few minutes after. The lawyer's secretary—Olsen, her name is—was on the telephone. Said she was trying to get the police. They'd all heard the shot, but nobody knew anything else. Except that the elevator had gone down."

"Mr. Perryman was supposed to be in it," a neat and blond young woman had told Shapiro. "I'm Mary Picket, Mr. Perryman's secretary. I brought the elevator up for him, you know. He hates waiting for elevators. Then—well, then I don't know what happened."

"You pressed the button to bring the elevator up, Miss Picket? When was that?"

"About five, like always. Mr. Perryman buzzed me, just the way he usually does about then. So I went out and punched the button. Sometimes it takes forever, almost, for it to come up. And, like I said, he hates to stand there waiting for it."

It hadn't taken forever this time. It had taken only a few minutes.

"So, when it came up and the door opened, I pressed the hold button and went to tell Mr. Perryman it was there."

"The hold button, Miss Picket?"

"It's just under the up and down signal buttons. Mr. Perryman had it put in especially, I think. So that once the elevator got to the sixth it would stay here until he was ready to use it. Otherwise, anybody could bring it down whenever they wanted, you know. And leave him waiting."

"Yes," Shapiro said. "Make it more convenient for him,

of course." And a good deal less convenient for those on lower floors, for whom it might also be quitting time. Of course, Perryman owned the building.

"How about the emergency stop button inside the elevator?" Nate asked Miss Picket. "Couldn't you just as well have used that to keep the elevator here for Mr. Perryman?"

Miss Picket smiled just perceptibly. "Well—there's a story that one of his secretaries before me pushed the emergency alarm button in there by mistake and it rang all over the building—they do, you know—and Mr. Perryman was so annoyed that he had this special hold button put on the wall."

"I see," Shapiro said. "So, the elevator door opened," he said, "and you went to tell Mr. Perryman. After you had set the hold button. When the door opened, Miss Picket, was the ceiling light on in the car?"

"Why," she said, "it must have been, mustn't it? I mean, it always is."

"You didn't notice whether it was. Just—well, assumed it was on as always?"

"I guess so. As soon as the door opened and I'd set it on hold, I went to tell him."

"And he went out right away?"

"Yes. After he'd said good night, of course. And I had one letter to finish. For him to sign tomorrow, you know. And then—well, then there was this strange sort of popping noise. Not loud, really. Just sort of a pop. Out in the corridor."

They were in Miss Picket's small office. The door was open. The office was half the width of the building from the two elevators. A small-caliber revolver doesn't make a very large bang, of course. And Miss Picket was, no doubt, concentrating on her typing.

It was one of the other girls—Helen Casby, who said she was Mr. Johnson's secretary—who had gone to check on the sound of the shot. Her office was nearer the elevators. Just across the corridor from them, in fact. The elevator was, from the indicator, already on the way down. But there was a "funny smell" in the corridor. "Sort of as if somebody had been shooting off firecrackers."

A fired revolver leaves an odor behind it; a revolver, almost certainly, since there was no ejected cartridge case in the blood on the floor of the elevator car. After the unconscious, still bleeding Russel Perryman had been removed by the ambulance attendants, Shapiro had looked.

"The lab boys are still going over it," Shapiro told Tony Cook. "Doubt if they'll find anything."

"Somebody just standing in the elevator," Tony said, "with the light off? Waiting for Perryman to come in and be shot? Knew it would be Perryman who came in, Nate?"

"Way it looks, doesn't it? On the way down, the car stopped at the third floor. I was waiting for it on the second."

"Stopped for somebody to get out," Tony said.

"Sure as hell nobody got in," Nathan said.

"Got out with blood on his shoes, probably," Tony said. "And ran downstairs and on his way."

"Probably," Shapiro said. "Unless the third's where he works, of course. Financial and sports departments, as I remember."

"And the photographers," Tony said.

Nathan agreed that the photographers were also on the third floor. "The lab boys are down there now," he said. "Looking for bloody stains."

"The good old bloody footprints," Tony said. "Only maybe our guy was careful not to step in it."

"Could be. Probably was. I avoided it. Got blood on my trousers when I was down beside him, trying to stop the bleeding. Also, there are no footprints in the blood on the floor of the elevator. Guess we'd better go down to the third and ask around."

They went down to the third floor in the functioning elevator. They did not have to wait long for it. By close to seven in the evening, the building had emptied.

Not quite, it turned out, on the third floor. There were

two men in the sports department, which was rather like the city room, only smaller. One of the men was reading copy; the other was at a typewriter.

"Something I can do for you?" the man reading copy asked. He was a heavy man, probably in his fifties. He had lost most of his hair. Shapiro told him who they were.

"Philip Carson," the heavy man told them. "And the genius over there is Andy Baruch. Only we call him Barney, of course. No relation, however, are you, Barney?"

Baruch said something that sounded like "Urk" and went on typing.

"Were you here around five o'clock this evening, Mr. Carson?" Shapiro said.

He sure as hell had been. "But not around one this morning," Carson said. "So I don't know anything about it, do I? Ten thirty in the morning until whenever the geniuses get their overnights in, so I can correct their spelling. And put their leads into English."

Baruch stopped typing and ripped a sheet of paper from the typewriter. He got up and shuffled several sheets together. He took them to Carson at the copydesk.

"Read all about it," he said. "You'll find it's in English, supposing you can read English. It says the Mets aren't going anywhere this year. And listen, pal, don't you think that 'genius' line is wearing sort of thin? He left four-five years ago and, far's I know, hasn't turned out to be Shakespeare yet. O.K.?"

Carson grinned up at him. He said, "O.K., Barney. On your way."

Baruch moved toward the open door of the sports office.

"Before you go, Mr. Baruch," Shapiro said, "did you see anybody getting out of the elevator on this floor a little after five this evening? Anybody you knew?"

"I wasn't here," Baruch said. "Got here around five thirty or so. The Mets took eleven innings to lose today. Right, Phil?"

"Nearer a quarter of six," Carson said. "Stopped for a quick one, I shouldn't wonder. What's this about somebody getting out of the elevator around five? Any reason somebody shouldn't?"

Shapiro said, "Thanks, Mr. Baruch," and, to Philip Carson, "Every reason why somebody should, Mr. Carson. Somebody who'd just shot Mr. Perryman."

Carson said, "Jee-sus Christ! Somebody *shot* the old boy?"

Shapiro nodded his head. Carson said he'd be damned and that it was a hell of a thing. Then he said, "Is the old boy dead?"

"In surgery, last we heard," Shapiro said. "Could be in intensive care by now, if he's lucky."

"That bad?" Carson said.

Shapiro said it seemed to be.

"Somebody's turning this goddamn place into a shooting gallery," Carson said.

Nathan Shapiro said it did sort of look that way and, "The elevator, Mr. Carson? Around five o'clock?"

"I was reading copy, not watching elevators," Carson said. "Sitting right here reading Brent's overnight on the Yanks. Not their year either, seems like."

Where Carson was sitting, he had his back to the open door, and hence to the elevator corridor. Yes, in answer to Shapiro's question, *right* there. Oh, around four he had knocked off long enough to go down to the lobby for a cup of coffee. Back in half an hour, at a guess. Put the page together for the sports final. Then went back to reading overnights. The copy'd gone along to the composing room, as usual. And now, as soon as he read Baruch's copy on the Mets, he was going to knock it off for the day and go home.

He sure as hell hadn't been watching the elevators at any time. They wouldn't have been much in use anyway. The "financial wizards" ducked out around four thirty, usually.

Shapiro and Cook stood up. They had turned toward the door, and Carson had picked up his thick pencil, when Tony thought of something. Just on the outside chance.

"This genius you and Mr. Baruch were talking about," he said. "The one who left four or five years ago and hasn't turned out to be a Shakespeare yet. Wouldn't have been a man named Mead, would it?"

"Brian Mead," Carson said. "He has turned out to be a playwright. Couple of hits on Broadway right now. Five years ago, somebody took an option on a play of his. Play about a tennis player. What he covered for us, mostly. Nowadays we use the services for tennis. And for baseball when the teams are on the road, come to that. We've been pulling in our horns, last few years. Not the way things used to be. The old boy's losing money, probably, but he's a stubborn old bastard. And people are still buying groceries."

Shapiro and Cook sat down again.

"This Mr. Mead," Shapiro said. "He work here very long, Mr. Carson?"

"Year or so," Carson said. "What's about Mead? Covered tennis for us for a while. Some football. Didn't know too much about football, but he got by. Got this option money and took off. Always wanted to write plays while he was on the staff here. Talked about it quite a lot. What's about him for you guys?"

"Probably nothing," Shapiro said. "A lot of the things they want us to check out aren't really about much of anything. Mead was here long enough to know his way around, I'd take it?"

"Around what? He was a savvy enough guy."

"Around the building, I guess," Shapiro said.

"You mean, could he find the men's room, Lieutenant?"

"Something like that. He could generally find his way around the building?"

Philip Carson supposed so. There was nothing particularly complicated about the Sentinel Building. He still couldn't make out what Shapiro was shooting at.

"Probably nothing," Shapiro said, and stood up again. Cook stood up with him. This time they went out of the sports department. Shapiro found a telephone.

Russel Perryman had survived surgery. He was now in intensive care. A small-caliber bullet had pierced his right lung. He was unconscious and in critical condition. He might make it; with a reasonable amount of luck, he probably would make it. It would be several days, at best, before he could be asked any questions.

"Odd coincidence about Mead," Tony said, as they waited for the elevator. "Of course, a good many writers start off on newspapers. As sportswriters, even. Take Broun. Take Pegler, for that matter."

Shapiro agreed that it was an odd coincidence about Mead, and supposed that a good many people went on from newspapers to other kinds of writing. He was glad to take Broun. Pegler was another matter. One has to draw the line somewhere.

"This young Perryman you talked to," Shapiro said, when they were on the street. "Get anything we can use?"

"Doesn't seem like a red to me," Cook said. "He is a member of Common Cause. Enough to convince a man like Sampson he's a commie, I suppose."

"No trouble finding him, I gather?"

"Had to wait a while. Didn't turn up at his apartment until around six."

"And finished work at four," Shapiro said. "Not all that far from here to Grove Street, is it? And if his father doesn't make it, I suppose his son inherits. Newspaper and supermarkets, probably."

"Yeah," Tony Cook said, "I've thought of that, Nate."

"Hard not to," Shapiro said. "Suppose we leave it to the night boys for now, Tony. Maybe they'll turn up something."

Tony Cook was entirely ready to leave it to the four-to-midnight. And the midnight-to-eight, for that matter. Willing enough to take a cab to Gay Street.

Nathan Shapiro took the subway to Brooklyn. It was seven forty-five by then, and Rose would have assumed he wasn't going to make it home for dinner. And she would have food warming in the oven on the off chance.

Tony's cab driver knew the general location of Gay Street, which in itself was a minor miracle. It had been a day notably short on miracles. When he was in his apartment on the floor above Rachel Farmer's, he telephoned down to her. He told her he was afraid he was going to be late.

"You are late," she told him. There was no special asperity in her voice. "Almost an hour late. And there's no use telling me that, after all, you're a cop. I know you're a cop. One who can't remember about telephones, apparently."

Tony said he was sorry. He said that he was upstairs and would come downstairs as soon as he'd had a shower.

"I've got the glasses on ice," Rachel said. "Since a quarter of seven, they've been on ice. Frozen in solid by now, the poor things probably are."

It took Tony Cook only ten minutes to shower and run an electric razor over his face and put on fresh clothes. And to snap on his shoulder holster with the offduty revolver in it. It was only a few minutes after eight when he knocked his signal on Rachel's apartment door. Which meant that he was only a few minutes more than an hour later than the time they had planned on.

Rachel wore a sleeveless white dress, which was appropriate to the weather. She had a short black sweater jacket lying on an arm of the sofa, which was appropriate to the season of the year, if not to the temperature. She had high-heeled white shoes on, which made her within a couple of inches of Tony's six feet. As they now and then mentioned to each other, they made a long couple. After several years, they still measured against each other in bed. Neither of them had shrunk.

Tony said he was sorry, and she said, "Aren't you always?" and they moved into each other's arms. Then Tony poured chilled Tio Pepe into Rachel's chilled glass and measured chilled gin and a token of vermouth over ice in a mixing glass, which had also been in the refrigerator and was almost too cold to touch. They clicked glasses and sipped. Tony lighted their cigarettes.

"Hugo's?" Rachel said.

If she liked. But it would be cooler at the Algonquin. "I stopped in at Hugo's for a beer this afternoon. They've decided it's fall and turned off the air conditioning. Anyway, turned it down. And the Algonquin was going by the thermometer, not by the month. Anyway, it was around noon."

"You find nice places to detect in," Rachel told him. "You and Nate, I suppose. About poor Mr. Claye, the rat?"

"Yes. A playwright at the Algonquin. A newspaperman on Grove Street."

"What I had for lunch," Rachel told him, "was a corned beef on rye. Thoroughly dried out. And a paper cup of patent coffee. During a ten-minute break."

Rachel, in addition to being a photographer's model and a model for painters, has been acting in segments of a TV series. She has what she calls "with" parts. The filming is being done in New York instead of in Los Angeles—or in San Francisco, where motorcars are constantly bouncing over the same street bump with a cable car in the background. Obviously, as Rachel insists, the same cable car.

They got to the Algonquin at nine, still in time for dinner. The Algonquin has an intermission between the dinner hour, which ends at nine thirty, and the supper hour, which starts around eleven. They had their second and third drinks at a table in the Oak Room, instead of, as usual, in the lounge.

There were few people in the Oak Room. Two of those still in the dining room were Mrs. Roger Claye and Brian Mead. They were at a corner table in the rear of the long room, not at one of those Robert reserves for people he would like to have noticed. Or, of course, for those who would like to be noticed.

Tony noticed the couple at the rather secluded table. He did not exactly stare at them, but for a moment he turned a little toward them.

"Friends of yours?" Rachel asked him.

"Just people who keep popping up a little," Tony said. "The woman is Mrs. Roger Claye."

"The widow Claye," Rachel said, and herself turned to look at Faith Claye and Brian Mead. "Looks from here as if she'd deserved better. And doesn't look too downhearted, does she? As a widow is supposed to. Already in public with another man. Tut, tut."

The waiter brought them food. Tony devoted himself to his plate. It was mildly interesting that Faith Claye and Brian Mead were again having dinner together, as they had the night before. It was worth making a note of, and Tony made a note of it in his mind. But he also noted that Rachel kept glancing at the couple at the corner table. He looked at her, and raised his eyebrows.

"It's only that I keep feeling I've met her somewhere," Rachel said.

"She lives on West Eleventh," Tony said. "You probably just passed her on the street."

"Probably," Rachel said. "Although I wouldn't think she's all that memorable. To a woman, anyway. And I pass hundreds of people on the street. Thousands, really. Without ever really seeing them."

"We all do," Tony said, and they ate their dinners. They were drinking their coffee when Faith and Mead walked by their table on the way out. They proved that people can walk by other people without really seeing them. Both of them had met Tony Cook within hours. Neither of them seemed wary of detectives.

Terry got Tony and Rachel a cab after a few minutes.

Terry didn't remember, when Tony asked him, anything special about the night before, except it was raining like hell and a lot of people had expected him to invent taxicabs. No, he didn't know Mrs. Roger Claye by sight. He had no idea whether she had been one of those who wanted him to conjure a cab out of rain-swept streets. Yes, sure he knew Mr. Mead; Mr. Mead lived there. No, he didn't remember him from the night before.

A taxi answered the shrill note of Terry's whistle. The driver knew where Gay Street was. Down in the East Village. Tony explained to him that he didn't know where Gay Street was and that it was west of Fifth Avenue, on which they were bound south. The driver said, "Sure, Mac. Like I said."

Rachel was quiet as they rode downtown. They had just turned into Ninth Street when she said, "It was at a party somewhere, I think. Down here somewhere, except that it feels like they were uptowners."

8

It was not until they were in bed, quiet again and with her head on his shoulder, that Rachel Farmer went on with that. Her voice was a little sleepy in his ear.

"It was at a party Arnie took me to," she said. "Not my kind of party and it was years ago. It wasn't really his kind of party either. Arnold Rather, dear. I've told you about him."

She had told him about Arnold Rather. Possibly not all about him, of course. Tony didn't even wonder much. The present was enough; the present was fine. There was no point in rummaging in the past. In either of their pasts, come to that. Tony, himself a little sleepy now, wondered how Arnie Rather came into anything. He said, "Yes, dear. At a party years ago. What at a party, child?"

"I met Mrs. Claye," Rachel said. "Maybe not really met her. It was rather a big party. Arnie was doing a number.

Two numbers, I think. He took me along. I don't think anything really came of Arnie's numbers in the end."

Whereupon, Rachel appeared to go to sleep. Drowsiness was understandable. It had been an active evening since dinner, as their evenings tend to be.

But something stirred in Tony Cook's mind. The stirring brought him fully awake. Arnold Rather? Doing numbers at a party. But wasn't Rather the one—?

"Arnold Rather," Tony said. "Wasn't he the guy who worked on the *Sentinel* once? Assistant music editor or something?"

Rachel awakened reluctantly. She said, "Maybe I did. Why? Oh, the *Sentinel!*"

"Yes," Tony said. "The place where people get shot."

"Arnie's a composer, really," Rachel said. "Mostly there's really a lot of money in writing music, or almost none at all. He's on the West Coast now, somebody told me. I haven't seen him for years. I never saw him very much, Tony. You're not going to be—?"

Tony kissed her an answer to that. He said, "He did work on the *Sentinel,* child? Several years ago? In their music department?"

"For about a year. He did a column on new recordings, and second-string concerts and things like that. It was only for about a year."

"But he did get to know people on the paper," Tony said. "Ever talk to you about them?"

"A little. After he got fired. Because the music department wasn't bringing in enough advertising. What they told him, anyway. Said that all Simpson cared about was the financial page. Stock quotations and things like that. And blasting away at—the way he put it—'anybody whose mind wasn't still in the stone age.' Of course, Arnie was really hipped on music then. Probably he still is. And he is—was then, anyway—pretty much a left-winger."

"Simpson?" Tony said. "Or could it have been Sampson? He's managing editor there now."

"Simpson-Sampson," Rachel said. "Yes, he was an editor. Managing editor sounds right. Anyway, Arnie didn't like him much. Said he was a typical red-neck. In a white collar. He was the one who junked the music department, and Arnie with it. Explains why Arnie felt the way he did, I suppose."

"Well," Tony said, "Mr. Sampson does seem like a rather—arbitrary man. I only talked to him a few minutes this morning. He doesn't seem to be very popular with the staff."

"He certainly wasn't with Arnie. But then, a lot of people weren't, when I knew him. He used to go on a lot about Nixon."

Tony said, "Yes, I'd suppose he would. Lots of people did, of course. I did myself. And how right we were, as it turned out."

Rachel said, "Mmm," in the cadence of one who is about to go back to sleep. But Tony was wide enough awake by now.

"It was Sampson who moved in on the music department," he said. "Because it wasn't paying its way?"

"And because only Jews wanted to read about music," Rachel said. "He said something like that to Arnie. Arnie's mother is Jewish, you know."

Tony hadn't known. He wouldn't have cared if he had. He didn't care much about Arnold Rather, come to that. But he was interested in people at the New York *Sentinel*.

"It was Sampson who made the decision about music coverage," he said. "Not the editor of the paper? A man named Wainwright?"

"Could be Arnie was wrong," Rachel said. "The way he thought it was. He did mention a man named Wainwright once or twice. Seemed to like him better than anybody else he ran into at the paper. Said he hadn't had much to do with him, but that he seemed like a good guy in a bad spot. Said this Wainwright man seemed to be a legend down there. A fading legend, Arnie said he seemed to be. Listen, Tony, is this a time for a chat? Or for you to go upstairs and go to sleep? Or?"

The "Or" seemed to present an alternative, and one for which Tony Cook was ready. It was some little, but exciting, time before he swung out of Rachel's wide bed, and put on clothes enough to go up to his own apartment in. (An apartment in Gay Street, just above Rachel Farmer's, was certainly more convenient.)

He had shirt and trousers on when his mind reverted to something of possible importance.

"This party Rather took you to," he said. "Was it a sort of audition party? For possible backers of a production in the theater?"

"You do harp, darling," Rachel said. "A girl needs her sleep. Yes, I think that's what it was. For a revue or something. But I don't think it ever came off."

"A party down here in the Village?" Tony said. "In a house on Eleventh Street, could it have been?"

She said a sleepy "Huh?" Then she said, "Yes, I think it could have been Eleventh Street. Or maybe Twelfth. Why don't you go upstairs and go to bed, Tony?"

Tony went upstairs and went to bed. He wondered who had been at the party at the Claye house, but he had pressed Rachel far enough. There can be issues in a man's life even more important than catching a murderer.

As he slipped toward sleep, Tony thought, a little dimly, of the other things he might have asked Rachel. Had Roger Claye been her host—and Arnold Rather's host, of course—at this party in West Eleventh Street—and had she met him? And had Rather, a man of leftist leanings, also met him? Had Brian Mead, sportswriter or ex-sportswriter and rising young playwright, been at the party? If Claye had been at the party, the auditioning party, at his own house, had Rather met him, and had sparks flown?

All trivial questions, probably, and Rachel would be

asleep by now. It had somehow got to be after midnight; he was due in the squad room at eight.

Usually, Tony has only to set an alarm clock in his mind. This night he also set the alarm clock on a table not too near his bed; not so near he would not have to get out of bed to shut it off. People can shut alarm clocks off in their sleep, if it is easy to reach clocks.

Tony Cook slept. Briefly, he dreamed about someone named Arnold Rather. The dream Rather was very ugly. He had large, ugly hands. He was also cross-eyed. Tony slammed a door on the dream Rather. The door hit Rather on his long, ugly nose. Tony's sleep became contented.

It was, however, unmercifully brief. His mental alarm clock and the material one went off more or less at the same time, which was seven o'clock. Tony growled at the real alarm clock as he got out of bed to shut it off. He showered while the coffee water came to a boil. He poured almost boiling water on the all-Colombian coffee in the Chemex. After two cups of it and a cigarette, he felt up to soft-boiling an egg and toasting a slice of bread. The telephone rang as he was buttering the toast.

Huh? The *Sentinel* office instead of the squad room? As soon as he could make it? And the lieutenant was on his way there?

O.K. He was on his way.

He did allow himself the egg and part of the slice of toast. And another cup of coffee. On his way downstairs, he did not allow himself the signal tapping on Rachel's apartment door. With any luck, she would still be asleep. Not, he trusted, dreaming of a man as ugly as Arnold Rather.

He had to wait only about thirty seconds for a downtown subway train at the Sheridan Square-West Fourth Street station. He was at the Sentinel Building at a quarter after eight. A patrol car was just arriving as he went into the building. But there had been one before it. Two uniformed patrolmen were in front of the elevators, one of which had an Out of Order sign dangling in front of it.

"Upstairs," one of the patrolmen said, after Tony showed his ID card. "Second floor."

Tony pinned his gold shield on as he went up the flight of stairs.

There were several men in the corridor outside the city room. They were looking down a side corridor at another uniformed policeman. This one was a sergeant, whom Tony knew slightly, but not enough to remember his name. Martinelli? Something like that. The sergeant was standing outside a door, and when Tony got to the door he saw it was marked "Men."

"Morning," the sergeant said. "Cook, isn't it? Sergeant Rossi. Old Slip station. They're inside." Well, thought Tony, I wasn't too far off. Headed in the general direction, anyway. Martini and Rossi. He went into the men's room. Lieutenant Daley of the precinct squad was there.

"Right at the end of the shift the squeal comes in," Daley said. "Wouldn't you know? Five minutes and I'd have been on my way. And not all that rush, it turns out. Clean miss, or damn near. What gives with these guys, anyway?"

It was the way things broke sometimes. Squeals come in at inconvenient times. And what did give with these guys today, Lieutenant?

"Attempted murder," Daley told Cook. "Around here, a man can't even pee in peace. Without getting shot at, I mean."

The men's room was fairly large. There were half a dozen urinals in a line, nearest the door. Beyond them, deeper in the room, there were four stalls. Against the wall opposite, there were four washbasins. A detective was scrambling around on the floor. He was under one of the washbasins. He came out and stood up. He said, "Got it!" on a note of triumph and held out to Daley a small piece of battered metal.

It was, Tony saw, what remained of a slug from a small-caliber gun, probably either revolver or automatic pistol. At a guess, a .22 or .25. And it was nothing to be triumphant about. It was distorted, flattened by its impact against something hard. Harder, obviously, than a man.

Yes. Of course. A large chip had been knocked from one of the wings of the urinal nearest the door. The slug had bounced away to lie under one of the washbasins.

"Saw what was coming and ducked, way we get it," Daley said. "Lucky bastard."

"Very," Tony said. "And just who was it, Lieutenant?"

"Guy named Sampson. Some kind of editor or something. Wait a minute." He took a notebook out of a pocket and looked at it. "Leroy Sampson," he said. "Managing editor, way I've got it here. Went on into what they call the city room. Where he's got his desk, I suppose. Not a very talkative guy. Said, 'All right. He missed. And I've got a paper to get out.' So—he's up to you guys. Damn shooting gallery around here, and you're welcome to it."

Tony Cook said, "Thanks," with no thankfulness in his voice, and started out of the men's room. Lieutenant Nathan Shapiro was just about to come into it.

"Sampson," Tony said. "Clean miss, apparently. Found the slug. Bashed up. Ballistics won't be happy. Sampson's gone back to his desk."

They walked the corridor toward the city room.

"Perryman's what they call 'stable,'" Shapiro said. "Which seems to mean he's still alive. Still in intensive care. Still unconscious. The captain's got Sanders standing by, but they won't let anybody into intensive care."

"Wouldn't be much point to it if they would," Tony said. "Not while the old boy's still dead to the world."

Shapiro said, "Mmm," agreeing to the obvious.

The city room was not as populated as it had been the morning before. Only a scattering of reporters were at their desks. Only two of them were using their typewriters. Two of the three desks which made up the city desk were occupied.

In the distant corner of the room, under a tall window, Leroy Sampson was sitting at his desk. He was looking at something on it. A rather burly blond man was standing by the desk, obviously waiting. As Cook and Nathan Shapiro walked across the big room toward Sampson's desk, the blond man took a sheet of paper held out to him by Sampson.

"O.K., Mr. Riley," Sampson said, as the two tall men from Homicide South stopped a few feet from the desk. "Two line six. Who've you got doing it?"

"Notson," the man called Riley said. "Fremont's day off."

Sampson nodded, and Riley left the desk and went back toward his own, which was the third of the three city desks.

Sampson looked up at Shapiro and Cook as they moved forward. The expression on his face was not friendly. His face was heavy-jawed. His eyes were a cold blue. He said, "Yes?" and made the word a demand.

"You're the one named Cook, aren't you?" Sampson said. "Bumbling around here yesterday morning, weren't you? After the red bastards shot Mr. Claye. And who're you?"

The last was to Shapiro, who told the belligerent man who he was.

"Shapiro, huh?" Sampson said. "And a lieutenant already?"

The "already" sounded like a challenge, and a slur. If it was a challenge, Nathan did not take it up. He said, "Yes, Mr. Sampson. I'm a detective lieutenant. We'd like you to tell us what happened."

"I damn near got killed is what happened. By one of those Communist bastards you let run around loose. And those nine old geezers make their decisions for." He added, "Lieutenant," again with contempt in his tone.

"We try not to let killers run loose," Shapiro said. He avoided adding, "Whatever their politics." Sampson's antagonism was, he thought, built in. There was no point in adding to it. "It'll help if you'll just tell us what happened."

"I've got a newspaper to get out," Sampson said. "Already told the other police officer about it. Why don't you ask him about it? Or don't you speak to each other?"

"We're from Homicide, Mr. Sampson. Supposed to get things firsthand when we can. Detective Cook and I are working on Mr. Claye's murder. And the wounding of Mr. Perryman, who's still unconscious, by the way. And so can't help us."

"You and a detective," Sampson said. "What's the matter with the chief of detectives?"

"Nothing, Mr. Sampson. We're working under his direction, of course. Following his instructions. Reporting to him when we have anything to report. Tell us about this morning, won't you? What happened in the washroom?"

"Like I said, I damn near got killed. Oh, all right. I'll go over all of it again. Not here, though. In my office. Come on and let's get it over."

He got up from the desk and walked toward them. It was evident they were supposed to get out of his way. They did. They followed him across the city room and through the corridor, past the ticker room, and into the other section of the second floor. He stopped at a door on the Broadway side of the building and used a key to unlock it. He went into the office, and Nathan and Tony Cook followed him.

His office was noticeably larger than the office of Jason Wainwright, editor of the New York *Sentinel*. His desk was bigger than Wainwright's. The window behind the desk was wider than Wainwright's window, and more light came through it. Sampson sat behind his desk. There was one other chair in the room. Sampson said nothing about either of them sitting on it, but Shapiro did anyway. Cook leaned against the wall and got his notebook ready.

"Got down here about five minutes of eight, as I do most mornings," Sampson said. "I've got a trained taxi driver picks me up every morning. So I went into the men's room, way I usually do. And got shot at. Don't knock that TV set over, Cook."

Tony Cook was against the wall beside a wide-screen TV set on a small table. He had put his notebook on it. He had had no intention of knocking the set over. He took his notebook off the top of the set and held it in his hand. Sampson stared across the room at him, as if expecting an oral response to his instruction. Probably, "Yes, sir. Thank you, sir." He didn't get it.

"You make a habit of going to the men's room as soon as you get down here, Mr. Sampson?" Shapiro asked.

"Pretty much, I guess. What the hell, Shapiro?"

"A habit that could be counted on, I mean. By, among others, somebody with a gun."

Sampson looked hard at Nathan Shapiro through very cold blue eyes. Nathan could see why Leroy Sampson was not notably popular with the people who worked under him. Shapiro waited.

"I suppose so," Sampson said, after a pause. "Anybody on the staff. Only there aren't any commies on my staff. You can be damned sure of that."

"I'm sure there aren't," Shapiro said. "You got to the office a few minutes before eight and went to the men's room, as you usually do. Then, Mr. Sampson?"

"I peed. I'd finished and zipped up and was about to wash my hands. Had turned toward the washbasin when I saw this glint. Something reflecting the light. And saw a hand reaching out of one of the cubicles, and the glint was coming off the gun this guy was holding—holding pointed at me."

"Just a hand? Not a face?"

"No face. Just a hand with a gun in it sticking out from behind a door opened just wide enough. A hand with a finger on a trigger. That what you want, Shapiro?"

"Just the picture," Shapiro said. "The cubicle—stall—nearest the urinals?"

"Second one down. Maybe eight-ten feet from where I was standing."

"You were lucky he missed at that distance," Shapiro said. "Of course, small handguns are tricky. Hard to aim."

"Lucky, hell," Sampson said. "Think I just stood there waiting to be shot? By the time he pulled the trigger, I was down on the floor. Caught myself on my hands, of course. I play tennis some, Shapiro. You play tennis, you learn how to fall. Something you wouldn't know about, probably. Not your people's line, is it?"

Shapiro supposed he was intended to pick that up, possibly with a list of names. Starting with Victor Seixas, probably, and ending with Solomon. He didn't.

"You dropped to the floor," he said. "Landing on your hands. He didn't take another shot at you?"

"No. Maybe thought he'd got me the first time. He just —scuttled away. I tried to get a look at him, but he was too quick for me. Just in time to see the door closing after him. Ran like the rat he was, Shapiro."

Of course, when a man has tried to kill you, you are justified in thinking of him as a rat.

"Like all of them," Sampson said. "All rats."

"That's all you saw of him?" Shapiro said. "Just a hand pushed out from behind a half-opened door?"

"With a gun in it, Shapiro."

"With a gun in it, Mr. Sampson. Nothing special about the hand you saw?"

"What the hell's supposed to be special about a hand? Except this one was holding a gun?"

"Nothing, probably. Oh, long fingers. Stubby fingers. A broad hand, or a narrow one. Nothing likely to be positive, I admit. Nothing we can go on, obviously. When he ran past you, Mr. Sampson. Did you get the feeling he was a big man? With a heavy tread, I mean. Or a smaller one? You used the word 'scuttled.' Doesn't sound like a heavy man, does it?"

"I told you. Sounded like a rat. Used to hear them down

south when I was a kid. In the barn on my father's farm. He used to have the farm niggers shoot them. Down in Alabama, that was."

There wasn't much of Alabama left in Sampson's accent, Nathan thought. Oh, it came out a little like "nigguhs." There was a good deal of Alabama left in Sampson's mind, although it had been eroded from his speech. All right, I've got my prejudices, too. And you don't have to go to an Alabama farm to find rats. There are more rats than people in New York City, at a guess.

"You went out into the corridor after you'd been shot at, Mr. Sampson. See anybody running down it? Toward the city room, maybe?"

"After I'd washed my hands, sure I went out of the washroom. Banged my hands up some when I landed on them. And the floor isn't all that clean."

He spread his hands out on the desk top as he said this. They were large hands, suitable to a rather large man. They did not look particularly banged up.

"Well," Shapiro said, "if that's all you can tell us, Mr. Sampson." He started to stand up. But halfway up, he said, "Yes, Cook?"

As usual, Tony had not realized he had looked like a man about to say something. As usual, Nate seemed to be psychic.

"I just wondered," Tony said. "With Mr. Perryman laid up, out of action, who runs the paper? Makes the important decisions. On, say, policy matters. If something big comes up? I suppose it would be Mr. Wainwright?"

"The paper pretty much runs itself, Cook. Day to day, that is. No policy matters, as you put it, likely to come up, that I know of. If any do, Burns and I can handle them."

"Burns?" Tony said.

"Ralph Burns, the business manager, Cook."

It was, from his tone, something anybody ought to have known, even a low-grade cop like Anthony Cook.

Cook said he saw.

"Not Mr. Wainwright, then?" Shapiro said. "I'd have thought that, as editor—"

"What he's called," Sampson said. "Handles the editorial page, sure. Old Wainwright's getting on. Has been for years, actually. And getting pretty wishy-washy, at that. Thing is, he's got this damn contract, apparently. And plans to hold the old man to it. Only, could be he's in for a surprise when Mr. Perryman is back on his feet. Yes, quite a surprise, it could be."

Shapiro repeated, "Surprise?" But Sampson only shook his head. He did smile a narrow smile.

9

Without consultation, Shapiro and Cook moved a few steps down the corridor, toward the south end of the floor. Sampson came out of his office, made sure the door had locked after him and went back toward the city room and, presumably, his corner desk.

"Well, I'll say it," Tony Cook said. "It takes all kinds."

"Why?" Nathan said, and Tony merely shook his head.

"All right," Nathan said. "He's got his prejudices. Anti-Semitic. Antiblack. Probably thinks Wallace is a great man. But the point is, somebody tried to kill him. Our point."

"He says somebody did, Nate."

Shapiro shook his head. He said, "The slug, Tony. And also, you could smell the powder. Somebody shot at him. And —somebody who knew his habits. So, somebody on the staff?"

"Or somebody on the staff who's passed the word," Cook said. "Or the taxi driver who brings him down here every morning. Passed the word, I mean. Or the elevator starter. Suppose there'll be another try at him, Nate?"

Shapiro agreed that that was possible. But not, probably, while he was at his desk in the city room. When he left, they might arrange to have somebody go with him, guard him.

"This commie angle they're all so hipped on," Tony said, as they walked down the corridor toward the adjoining offices of Peter Simms and Jason Wainwright, associate editor and editor of the New York *Sentinel*. "Claye, Perryman, now Sampson. All pretty extreme right-wingers. Not likely to be popular with left-wingers. And there are some pretty fanatical kids on the left, Nate. Try to kill people to save redwood trees. Of course, they're pretty much on the West Coast."

"Except local fighters for Puerto Rican independence," Shapiro said. "And a few nutsy Zionists. We've got our share, Tony. However—" He let it hang there.

The doors of most of the small offices on either side stood open; the offices were not occupied. The door of the office in which Roger Claye had been killed was closed. There was a police seal on it. For no really apparent reason, Shapiro thought. Whatever useful had been in there was no longer there. And, apparently, Saturday was a quiet day at the *Sentinel*. No editorials being written.

"By the way," Tony said, when they were close enough to the Wainwright and Simms offices to see that the doors of both were closed, "you did tell me once that you used to play tennis, didn't you?"

"When I was a lot younger," Nathan said, his sad voice appropriate to vanished youth. "Public courts. Prospect Park. Why, Tony?"

Tony Cook merely smiled in answer.

"Oh, all right," Nathan said. "I get your point."

"Come as a surprise to Mr. Sampson," Tony said. "Like it would have to Adolf Hitler."

It was Tony who knocked on the door of Jason Wainwright's office. There was no response from inside it. But when he knocked again, the door of Simms's office opened and Simms stood in it. He said, "Oh, it's you two. About the near miss this time, I suppose. Not guilty, gentlemen."

He held the door open, as an invitation. They went into the office.

"So you know about Sampson," Shapiro said.

"News spreads," Simms told him. "After all, news is our business around here. Supposed to be, anyway. And before you ask, I knew about the old boy's habit of going to the head before he went to his desk. For the precautionary pee, as it was generally called. So, at a guess, did everybody on this floor. And I've got nothing against Roy. I don't work under him. And I don't own a gun, Lieutenant. Wouldn't have one of the damn things around. So?"

"All right," Shapiro said. "So nothing much, Mr. Simms. Mr. Wainwright isn't around, apparently?"

"Never on Saturdays," Simms said. "On Saturdays, I man the fort. To write a sob editorial if a president gets shot. If he's the right party, that is. If he's a Democrat, of course, it's about the breakdown of law and order, growing out of the permissiveness encouraged by past Democratic administrations. Too bad, but they had it coming sort of thing. Hogwash either way, of course."

Shapiro said, "Mmm."

"All right," Simms said. "I'm flippant about sacred matters. Comes of being a pro, Lieutenant. Same as you are, come to that."

Shapiro said, "Mmm," again.

"But not about our local crime wave," Simms said. "Don't get me wrong. Wainwright isn't here. Probably at his hotel, having breakfast at a human hour for once. Or even, maybe, gone up to his place in the country. Where his wife and he used to spend weekends, and most summers. Doesn't go up there much anymore."

"You and Mr. Wainwright are friends, I gather," Shapiro said.

"Because I know something about his habits? Yes, we are. Matter of fact, he makes working here bearable for me. Fine man. Damned good newspaperman, Jase is. For all they've pretty much frozen him out since Perryman took over."

"What we wondered about a little," Shapiro said. "We've been talking to Mr. Sampson, you see. About his narrow escape this morning. But, other things sort of came up."

"I can imagine," Simms said. "Also, that you brought them up, Lieutenant. I've been asking around about you a little, Shapiro. Our district man at headquarters has filled me in. He's quite a fan of yours, Lieutenant."

Shapiro reverted to "Mmm." This time it had a trace of astonishment in it, even of incredulity. Tony Cook looked at him, but kept his smile to himself.

"These other things that happened to come up," Simms said. "About Jase Wainwright, I gather. Want me to guess about them, Lieutenant?"

He could if he liked, Shapiro told him.

"Not really guessing," Simms said. "Not part of the team, Wainwright isn't, according to our managing editor. Should have retired years ago. A doddering old man. Not up to much, nowadays. Lives in the past. That about it?"

"Something like that, Mr. Simms."

"Well, Jason is getting along. Late seventies somewhere. Quite a way beyond retirement age, granted. And nothing wrong with his mind. Still can think circles around a man like Sampson. Around old Perryman, too. Around me, come to that. The trouble is—well, he still believes in newspapers. In the *Sentinel,* especially. Remembers it the way it used to be. When old Mason owned it. Oh, it was for the Wall Street boys then, way it is now. But you got news in the news columns in those days. What Jason tells me, anyway. Before my time."

He stopped and shook a cigarette out of his pack. He held the pack out to Nathan Shapiro, who said, "Thanks, not just now." Simms raised his eyebrows toward Tony Cook, who shook his head.

"Wainwright can be quite eloquent about the good old days," Simms said. "Fact is, he should be working on the *Chronicle*. Had several offers to go up there, I think. Not that he ever talked about it but—well, things get around in the trade. Take our man Fremont. Does rewrite. Never gets a byline. Sampson doesn't believe in bylines. But everybody in town knows about Fremont. Knows he's tops. Knows if there's a big story, he's the man who wrote it. And why he sticks to the *Sentinel* nobody knows. Maybe for old times' sake. Like Wainwright. I wouldn't know."

"You stick around yourself, Mr. Simms."

"Not for long," Simms said. "I've got an offer from the *Chronicle*. Not an associate editor, or anything like that. Writing editorials. Editorial articles, as Jason calls them. Chance to get on their editorial board in a couple of years, maybe."

"You're taking the offer?"

"Probably. Not going anywhere here. Only—well, I hate to leave old Jason to the wolves. Not that I can scare off many wolves. Not the kind we have around here. But one of these days, Jason's going to retire."

"And you, I suppose, would take over the job as editor, Mr. Simms."

Simms laughed. There was no amusement in his laughter. He dragged deeply on his cigarette and stubbed it out. He stubbed it out very thoroughly. He looked at Shapiro for several seconds and then shook his head.

"Not a chance," he said. "No more than the snowball. The traditional snowball. Sampson and Burns, our esteemed business manager, would see to that. Hell, I'm a Wainwright man. Rumor going around they, and Mr. Perryman, of course, had picked Claye. Somebody knocked that plan out of kilter night before last."

He stopped suddenly.

"And don't be getting ideas, Lieutenant," he said. His voice was peremptory; it was as if he gave an order. "Jason doesn't need the job. He can retire any time, at full salary. Like—oh, like a Supreme Court justice. Stipulated in this famous contract of his. The one Perryman had to take over when he bought the paper. So don't get any ideas about Wainwright."

"I wasn't getting any," Shapiro said. "Not about anybody, so far."

"This left-wing fanatic, Lieutenant? The way Perryman, Sampson et al think it is?"

"Possibly," Shapiro said. "Yes, Cook?"

Tony is no longer really surprised by that. It does sometimes come a little suddenly. This time he was ready.

"Mr. Sampson seems to have a great deal of say around here," Tony said. "Of course, I don't know much about newspaper setups, but isn't that unusual? For a managing editor to, way it looks, be pretty much running things?"

"Varies from paper to paper," Simms said. "Most I've worked on, the M.E. just runs the news side. The editor makes policy, which is the policy the owner sets, of course. Yes, Roy Sampson has more influence than most. In a way, he does run the show. The way the owner wants it run. And Perryman is a big-business man. Thinks—well, the way most industrialists think. So did Lester Mason, I suppose. But Mason, from what I hear, was a newspaperman. From way back. Yes, Mr. Cook, Sampson is pretty important around here. Good many papers, they'd call him something else. Executive editor, probably. Matter of terminology."

"Yes, I see," Shapiro said. "Cook and I both gathered Sampson doesn't think highly of Mr. Wainwright. Of his competence. Matter of fact, he said Mr. Wainwright is wishy-washy. Term he used. Apparently you don't find him that, Mr. Simms."

"Typical of Sampson," Simms said. "Saying that, I mean. Couldn't be more wrong. Thing is, Wainwright knows there are at least two sides to questions. Issues. Knows which side he's on, all right. But knows there is another side. And that everybody on that side doesn't have to be either a crook or a jackass. Sampson doesn't. For him there's only one truth, and it comes direct from God. Well, anyway, from the sixth floor. By way of Alabama. One of the be-kind-to-niggers-long-as-they-know-their-place boys. If they don't, they're probably commies. All whites should be able to buy any gun they want. To protect themselves. You probably know the type."

"And there's an international conspiracy among Jewish people to take over the world," Shapiro said. "One I haven't got in on, apparently. Yes, I know the type, Mr. Simms. Isn't limited to the South."

"No," Simms said. "A little more virulent there, maybe. Or maybe not. And being rational isn't regional either, I suppose. But you're not here to talk philosophy, are you, Lieutenant?"

"No," Shapiro said. "To find a killer."

"Then," Simms said, "you're looking in the wrong place, don't you think?"

"It looks that way," Shapiro said. "Mr. Wainwright is off every Saturday, I take it?"

"Yes. We work a five-day week here. Didn't use to be that way. First paper I ever worked on, it was six days and Saturday night to get out the Sunday morning paper. That wasn't in New York. The Guild stopped that sort of thing. Drove old Mason crazy, their moving in did. What Jason tells me, anyway. Mason started a backfire. Company union, affectionately known as the Loyal Order of Catspaws. Trouble was, his union hung onto the Guild's coattails. Very disappointing to the old boy, I gather. Hated to bow to the inevitable. But did, in the end. As I said, he seems to have been a newspaperman."

The connection was not as clear to Nathan Shapiro as it evidently was to Peter Simms, to whom being a newspaperman was apparently similar to holding a degree of nobility. It was not germane.

"This day-off business," Shapiro said. "You get to pick them?"

"Goes by seniority, more or less," Simms said. "And, to a degree, by the requirements of the job. Everybody wants Saturday, of course, to go with Sunday. Saturday's a dull day, nowadays. Stock markets closed; people get out of town. Our kind of people, anyway. Circulation drops way down. Advertising with it. Not that either is very sensational these days."

"Will the end of Claye's column bring circulation down further, Mr. Simms?"

Simms shrugged his shoulders. He said, "Could be. Probably he had a following. Syndicate following, anyway. But who knows? Could leave Perryman in the black; could put him in the red. Deeper in the red, could be. One reason I'll probably take up the *Chronicle*'s offer. Matter of permanence, call it."

"That bad, you think?"

"Maybe not. You'd have to ask Ralph Burns about that. I just work here." And then, "Yes, son," in response to a knock on his door.

An office boy came in with the first—the Home—edition of the New York *Sentinel* under his arm. He put a copy of the paper on Simms's desk and, in response to a gesture, handed a copy to Nathan Shapiro.

The attempt on Leroy Sampson's life did not rate a streamer. It did get a two-column headline and the right-hand column of the front page.

The headline read:

EDITOR FOILS ASSAILANT'S
ATTEMPT ON HIS LIFE

Shapiro folded the paper and put it in a jacket pocket. Perhaps he would, in time, get around to reading about Leroy Sampson's narrow escape from death.

There was another knock on Simms's door. It was another office boy. He carried a bundle of mail. He started to put it down on Simms's desk.

"No, son," Simms said. "Goes to Mr. Gilbey. Third office up, on your left."

The boy said, "Yes, sir," and carried the mail out again.

"Keep changing office boys around here," Simms said. "He's a new one, to me anyway. What he's got is letters to the editor. Viewing with alarm the growing something or other. Congratulating the *Sentinel* on its firm stand for the free enterprise system. Frank Gilbey will sort this batch out. Throw them in the wastebasket or pass them along to Jason on Monday. Some of them we print, after fixing up the spelling."

The ringing of the telephone on his desk interrupted him. He said, "Simms. Yes, Roy," and listened for several seconds. Then he said, "O.K., if you and Burns want it. You checked with Wainwright?" He listened again. Then he said, "O.K. It'll be coming up. Sure, reign of terror ought to do it. Only, Roy, I'll send it out. You'll see it in proof."

He hung up.

"Have to get to work," he told Shapiro and Cook. "Mr. Sampson and Mr. Burns think we ought to have an editorial about all this. Front page, no less. Reign of terror detected at the *Sentinel,* the defender of our liberties. Further evidence of the breakdown of law and order. Sampson says he's been in touch with Jason—only he said he'd 'contacted Wainwright'—and that Wainwright approves. So, unless you two—? They do want it for the next edition."

"We won't bother you anymore, Mr. Simms. Taken up a good deal of your time already."

Simms's telephone rang again just as they reached the door. He said, "Simms," and listened. Then he used the handset to beckon them back. Then he said, "All right, Ed. Caught them. I'll pass it on." He replaced the receiver.

"Ed Riley," he said. "The city editor. He's got a letter he

thinks you'd better see. A crank letter, only he thinks maybe not."

Shapiro said, "Thanks." Peter Simms was winding paper into his typewriter as they went out of his office.

Ed Riley was the burly blond man they had earlier seen standing at Sampson's desk. His voice, when he greeted them, listened to their names and gave his own, was softly out of proportion to his bulk.

"Probably just a crank letter," he said. "We get them every so often. Sometimes they come in red ink. Anyway—"

He held an envelope out toward Shapiro, holding it gingerly between his fingernails. "Only," he said, "I'm afraid the horse is already stolen, Lieutenant. My prints all over it, probably. No way of knowing, had I?"

"No way, of course," Shapiro said, and took the envelope. He handled it by the edges, although probably the horse had been stolen. Post-office clerks would have left fingerprints.

The typewritten address was: "Edmond Riley, Esq." The envelope was the prestamped kind, obtainable from post offices. Shapiro used the eraser of a pencil to slide the single folded sheet out of the small envelope. The sheet was of standard typewriter paper. There was no heading. The message was typed. Pica type; no sign of misalignment of keys immediately apparent. It read: "The rat Claye is only for starters. We will strike again. And again. Until we rid the world of people like you. Hitler-like enemies of humanity."

It was signed, still in typescript: "The Enforcers."

"Just a crank letter," Riley said. "Case like this brings them out of the woodwork. I'm telling *you*."

"Yes," Shapiro said. "We get a good many, of course. Claiming what they call 'credit' for bombs and murders. Confessing to crimes to get their names in the papers and on the air. We know the world is full of nuts, Mr. Riley."

"Probably half a dozen more in today's letters to the editor," Riley said. "People hoping to get them printed in the column we call 'The Public Mind.' Gone along to Gilbey to be sorted out."

Shapiro said, "Mmm." He looked again at the envelope. Postmarked Grand Central Station, New York. Dated P.M. the day before. Addressed to Edmond Riley, Esq.

"Many come addressed this way?" he asked Riley.

"First one ever, far's I can remember," Riley said. "Usually, just to the editor. Sometimes to Wainwright, as editor. Get the name from the masthead. Try to make it look personal, figuring it will get more attention that way."

Shapiro said he saw. Masthead? He took the first edition of the *Sentinel* out of his pocket. It was a thin paper of twenty pages. Editorials in the first section, page nine. The masthead. Top of the left-hand column. "The New York Sentinel Corporation; Russel D. Perryman, President." And, in descending order: "Jason Wainwright, Editor. Leroy Sampson, Managing Editor. Peter Simms, Associate Editor."

That was all.

"I see you're not on the masthead," Shapiro said to the burly city editor.

"Don't get down to city editors," Riley said. "Not on this totem pole."

"Then?"

"Yes," Riley said, "I wondered too, Lieutenant. Of course, everybody else in the trade knows the name of the city editor here. But, well, I wondered too. Very specific, isn't it? And spelled right, too."

"Riley?"

"Sometimes they get the *e* in the wrong place—with two *l*s, of course," Riley said. "And a *u* for the *o* in my first name."

"Addressed to you, personally, it might get quicker attention?" Shapiro said.

Riley smiled, approving an apt student. He said he had thought of that. Why he had thought the lieutenant might want to give it his own quick attention.

Shapiro took the typed message, the typed boast and

threat, out of the pocket he had put it in. On a cursory examination, there were no evident irregularities; nothing that would, on comparison, identify the typewriter on which the message had been written. No filled letters, no letters out of alignment. But a matter for experts, of course. Nathan Shapiro does not regard himself as an expert in anything except, perhaps, the use of a handgun. Pressed, he will admit he is reasonably good with a handgun.

Still, he might make a start for the lab boys.

"A lot of typewriters here in this room, aren't there?" he said.

"Twenty or so," Riley said. "I never counted."

He looked around the big city room. Only a few of the many desks were occupied. Typewriters had been folded into half a dozen of the desks. "At least twenty," Riley said. "Most of the boys and girls are downstairs drinking coffee. We pretty much duck after the Home goes to bed. Yes, at least twenty typewriters. And in the building, maybe a couple of hundred. I know what you're thinking Lieutenant. But I doubt it like hell."

"You're probably right," Shapiro said. "Still."

"Knew my name," Riley said. "Knew his way around here. Even knew Boss Sampson's habits. Oh, I get your point. Want to start with mine? How does it go again?"

Shapiro told him how the threatening message went. Riley swiveled to face the typewriter on its stand beside his chair, and typed. His fingers were quick on the keys. Several spaces below the words "The Enforcers," he typed, "Riley, city desk." He handed the sheet to Shapiro. The paper was grayish, not the clear white of the paper on which the message had come.

"All of them?" Riley said, and waved a hand around the room.

"It might help," Shapiro said, to which Riley said, "Jesus!" Then, with his soft voice a little raised, he said, "Notson. You up?"

The reporter named Notson, who was reading the first edition of the New York *Sentinel,* said, "Yeah," and came over to the city desk.

"Give the police a hand," Riley said. "Type this out on everybody's typewriters, starting with your own. Keep the sheets separate, and identify the typewriter you used for each one. O.K.? Like this."

He gave Notson the carbon he had made of his own copy of the threatening message. Notson read it and said, "Jesus H. Christ!"

"Yes," Riley said. "And in the new lead for the Night."

Notson said, "O.K.," and went back to his typewriter.

"I can do some of them," Tony Cook said. "Touch may be different."

Shapiro agreed that that would be a good idea, and that the touch wouldn't matter as far as he knew. If the lab boys thought it would, the lab boys could do their own typing.

"Sit down," Riley said, and Shapiro sat in a chair at one end of Riley's desk. He took a pack of cigarettes out of a pocket, but Riley shook his head.

"Better go out in the hall if you want to smoke," Riley said. "No smoking in the city room. Boss Sampson's rule, since he gave them up himself. Rule doesn't apply to you, of course. Still, upset the old boy."

Shapiro put the pack back in his pocket.

"Quiet here on Saturdays," Riley said. "A third of the staff gets this as their day off. I go along after we put the Night to bed. So does Mr. Sampson, although he may stick around this afternoon to make sure this editorial he wants on the front page gets on the front page."

Shapiro nodded his head to show he had heard. Then he said, "By the way, is David Perryman one of the city staff who gets Saturday off?"

"Sure," Riley said. "The owner's son, what else? Not that he asked for it. He's a good kid. It just—well, sort of worked out that way."

"By way of Mr. Sampson?"

"Well," Riley said, "most things around here do, Lieutenant. In one way or another. As you may have gathered. Not that I'm not all for Dave getting Saturday off. He's a damn nice kid. And turning out to be a good rewrite man. Also, he called in a while back. Gone home from the hospital. Said his old man seems to be holding his own, thanks to blood transfusions. Seems Dave was a donor last night."

Shapiro said that they, also, had heard that Russel Perryman's condition had stabilized. He added that Homicide South had a man standing by.

"Could be he knows who shot him," Riley said.

Shapiro agreed it could be and said he hoped it would be. His voice, however, did not reflect too much hope. "Dark in the elevator," he explained. "He was coming in from a lighted corridor. And I don't suppose he had much time. Ever hear of a gang calls itself 'The Enforcers?' "

Riley never had. "They keep on sprouting up," he said. "Making righteous noises and blowing people up, kidnapping people, shooting people. To create a new society which won't cut down redwood trees. Black Panthers, Weathermen, all kinds. Come to that, even your people have a terrorist gang. Runs in the human animal, I suppose. But no Enforcers I've ever heard of."

Neither had Nathan Shapiro. He asked directions to the nearest telephone booth.

He would have to go down to the lobby floor to find one, Riley told him. Or, he could use any of the phones in the city room. He could dial 9 and then his number. "This one," Riley said, and pointed to the phone on his desk. "As long as you don't tie it up too long. District men'll be calling in, maybe."

Shapiro said he'd use one of the others, and went to one of the unoccupied desks. The instrument there had earphones, which Shapiro didn't use. He got Headquarters. O.K., they'd send up for some typed sheets for comparison.

Yes, they'd find the precinct detective who'd be holding them. Sure, they'd switch him over.

Captain Rosenwald, commanding the detachment responsible for observation of terrorist activities and the tactical force which, as needed, did more than observe them, had never heard of an organization calling itself The Enforcers. Which didn't mean that one didn't exist. "They keep coming out of the woodwork," Captain Rosenwald told Lieutenant Shapiro, who already knew that they kept coming out of the woodwork, although perhaps not so fast as they had a few years before. O.K., he'd appreciate it if Rosenwald would shop around. Yes, it was yesterday that The Enforcers had emerged from the woodwork. Sure, The Enforcers might be one man or, for that matter, one woman. He did remember that a kidnapper in Georgia had been the "General"—or perhaps "Colonel"—of a purging army which did not exist. Yes, if Rosenwald turned up anything, he'd be at Homicide South.

Tony Cook was still typing, using one machine after another. So was the reporter Notson.

Shapiro, obeying rules, went out to the corridor to have a cigarette. He had just lighted it when Leroy Sampson came out of the city room. He did not appear to see Shapiro. He was wearing a suit jacket and, a little unexpectedly, a hat. He went to the door to the staircase and through it. He looked, Nathan thought, like a man on his way home. He hadn't, evidently, waited to approve Simms's editorial about the conspiracy against the New York *Sentinel* and the newspaper's vigorous stand for law and order. To say nothing of free enterprise.

Nathan Shapiro is inclined to favor both, but not especially as slogans. Slogans can be so easily perverted. He is also in favor of motherhood, provided it is voluntary.

10

IT WAS a little after noon when Cook and Shapiro left the Sentinel Building. A detective from the lab had collected the original of The Enforcers' message, marked for identification, and a large handful of copies of it. There had turned out to be twenty-two typewriters in the city room and eight more in the part of the second floor occupied by editorial writers. They did not get samples from Simms's typewriter or from that of Jason Wainwright. The doors to both those offices were closed. They left the typewriters on the floor above—those in the sports department and the financial department—for later. (Along with those in the business office and the advertising department, and those used by the syndicate and those on the sixth floor. Newspaper plants are rife with typewriters.)

A little after noon is time for lunch for policemen who have had to get up early. Tony Cook mentioned this to

Nathan Shapiro when Shapiro came out of a telephone booth on the lobby floor with the report that Russel Perryman's condition was unchanged; that he was still unconscious and remained on the critical list.

Nathan agreed it was time for lunch. But since they would have to go uptown anyway, to check in at Homicide South, he thought they might as well stop off and have a word with David Perryman.

Tony raised eyebrows of inquiry.

"He may have a typewriter at home," Shapiro said. "Also, if his father doesn't make it, he'll probably inherit the paper. We'll have to check on that after lunch."

They walked through Canal to the station of the IRT subway and rode up to Sheridan Square. They reached the Grove Street house just in time to meet David Perryman coming down the steps.

Perryman had a lunch date uptown, but—well, all right. If it wouldn't take too long.

He led them into the house, and they followed him up to his apartment on the second floor. The apartment turned out, to Shapiro's eyes, to be unexpectedly neat for the apartment of a young bachelor on a Saturday morning. Especially, Shapiro thought, for a young bachelor living in Greenwich Village. (Which was, he admitted to himself, sheer prejudice, to which Brooklynites are not immune.)

Yes, Perryman had heard that somebody had taken a shot at Boss Sampson and missed him. He had heard it on the radio news at ten o'clock. He had not heard of the threatening letter Edmond Riley had received in the morning mail. "Somebody sure has it in for us," David said. No, he had never heard of a group calling itself "The Enforcers." "Enforcing what?" he said, which was a question neither Shapiro nor Cook could answer.

Yes, he had a typewriter. All right, he was trying to write pieces. For the *New Yorker* and—O.K.—*The Village Voice*. And no, he hadn't had any luck yet with either. But he knew a guy who'd sent forty-odd pieces to the *New Yorker* before he sold one. "And then he sold around a hundred." Of course, that had been years back. Sure, they could use his typewriter, but what the hell for? For comparison with what? "Hell, let me guess, Lieutenant. For Christ's sake!"

"We're making a collection," Shapiro told him.

Perryman's typewriter was an electric portable and looked new. Cook, not used to portables, had trouble with the spacing, but finally got a specimen line: "The quick brown fox jumps over the lazy dog," which has the advantage of utilizing all the letters in the English alphabet and is helpful for those learning the touch system.

Perryman went downstairs with them. It was Tony who suggested, after young Perryman had hailed a taxicab and gone off in it, that they might as well have lunch at Hugo's, since it was nearby.

Hugo's French Restaurant is on Sixth Avenue between Ninth and Tenth, a block below where Charles French Restaurant had flourished for some fifty years, had become a meeting place and a landmark and, several years ago, had gone out of business. Hugo's, to some slight degree, has taken its place. Charles, originally owned by a Hungarian, had been considerably more French. It was a short walk from Grove Street to Hugo's, and Cook and Nathan Shapiro walked it without conversation. It was a little before one when they reached it.

The bar was just inside the entrance, and it was well occupied. On Saturday afternoons in restaurants like Hugo's, New Yorkers who drink, drink early. Saturday is a day of rest.

A man of medium height and muscular build pushed a barstool back and slid off it. Standing, he finished a drink. He put bills on the bar and the barman said, "Thank you, sir." Momentarily, the muscular young man faced Cook and Shapiro. He said, "Hi again," to Tony Cook and went past them and out into Sixth Avenue.

"Our Mr. Mead," Tony said. "Brian. Playwright. The one who took Mrs. Claye to the theater night before last. Before she was a widow. Mead's up early this morning. This time yesterday he—oh. Almost forgot. He and Mrs. Claye were dining together at the Algonquin last night. Seen by me and Rachel."

"Mmm," Shapiro said. "We're not far from Eleventh Street, are we?" Then he said, "Two, please," to a hostess in a sleek black dress. The hostess was also sleek, but Tony regarded her with mild disapproval. It was not until they were seated at a table for two against a wall that Tony commented. "Sure miss Charles," Tony said. "Always had men for waiters there. Now every place is getting sort of like Schrafft's."

The menus were large. Tony ordered minute steak, rare, and a beer. Nathan settled for a glass of milk and a plain omelet. He thought of a glass of sherry, but rejected the thought. It was the sort of place where the sherry would be what they called "dry." Even if the waiters were women.

Tony's beer arrived promptly. He sipped from the glass.

"Of course," he said. "The Claye house is more or less just around the corner."

Shapiro nodded his agreement to the location of the Claye house.

"And the Village is still a stamping ground for people like Mead. Not as much as it used to be, when I was a kid down here. But still."

Again, Nathan nodded agreement, his agreement including, apparently, the "still."

Nate was not, Tony thought, in a communicative mood. Probably he was ruminating, which would mean he had a theory. Or might mean that he was not interested in Brian Mead's rather early appearance in Greenwich Village and his quick finishing off of what Tony took to be a manhattan.

Tony drank beer. Nathan Shapiro lighted a cigarette. He usually waited for a cigarette until after he had eaten. Which didn't mean anything.

They had to wait almost half an hour for food, which

led Tony to regretful acceptance of the probability his minute steak would not be rare. Or, of course, the broil chef might have a stack of steaks to do. Only, there weren't all that many lunchers in the restaurant. It was not really likely all of them were ordering minute steaks, leaving a cook behind a stack of them.

Food came, finally. But it was after two when they had finished their coffee. Tony had had a second beer by then, in preparation for the warmth outside. It was staying very warm for early September. But, of course, it often did. The weather was not breaking any rules; technically, it was still summer.

They had just paid their checks and were waiting for the waitress to bring back change when they heard a patrol car's siren wailing outside. At a guess, it had turned off Sixth Avenue into Tenth Street. Perhaps some amateur bomb makers had managed to blow up another town house? No—if they could hear the siren, they would have heard an explosion. A hit-and-run driver, probably. Or somebody holding up a nearby liquor store.

They had just stepped outside Hugo's when another cruise car went fast up Sixth Avenue, its roof light flashing and its siren screeching. It turned right into Tenth Street. Then, from some distance, there was the sound of another siren. Going down Fifth, probably. And, from beyond the library which had once been a courthouse, there was the gulping sound of an ambulance. The ambulance from St. Vincent's slowed as it came to Sixth and blared anger at other traffic before it crossed on a red light.

All hell had apparently broken loose somewhere. Tony said as much to Nathan Shapiro.

"Or," Nathan said, "somebody's seen somebody on a fire escape and thinks he's seen a burglar. But—" He let it hang on the "but" for a moment. Then he said, "May as well check it out, I suppose. Long as we're down here."

He went back into the restaurant. He was gone briefly.

"Man's been shot in the Square," he said, when he came out. "Sitting on a bench, according to the squeal. Long as we're here." He started to walk down Sixth, rather rapidly. Tony walked with him. Trouble with being on the squad, you didn't get homicides one at a time. Murders overlap. They walked through Ninth to Fifth Avenue; walked past the Ninth Street entrance of the Fifth Avenue Hotel. When they could look down Fifth toward Washington Square Park, they saw the backs of a huddle of people beyond the arch, and the fronts of patrolmen keeping them there.

They walked even faster down Fifth, across Eighth Street.

They had to push their way through the cluster of spectators, who were watching what there was to watch from a distance fixed by uniformed patrolmen. What they were watching was a police photographer taking pictures and a wheeled stretcher on a paved walk beside a row of benches with two ambulance attendants standing beside it.

The photographer's pictures were of a body stretched out on one of the benches.

The patrolman nearest said, "Hey you!" as Shapiro and Cook wriggled out of the thickening crowd of curious. "Where you think you're going?"

Shapiro's badge showed him who they were and where they were going. They went on, although it was not really their business. Except that killings in the southern part of the Borough of Manhattan are. And this was a killing. If the body on the park bench had been a live body, it would have been in the ambulance, on its way to the emergency ward of St. Vincent's Hospital. What they had was a DOA.

And what they had was Mr. Leroy Sampson, managing editor of the New York *Sentinel*. They had him dead, but still seeping blood, on a park bench in Washington Square Park, near the western side of the park. People were at the windows of a hotel across Washington Square West, looking down on the dead man, and on the lawmen death had brought to the Square.

Lieutenant Leonard Richardson of the precinct detective

squad said "Hi" to Shapiro and Cook. He said, "Didn't take you guys long, did it?"

"Happened to be down this way," Shapiro told him. "Shot, was he? A man named Sampson, he was. Worked on the *Sentinel.*"

"Yeah," Richardson said. "And had a press card to prove it. Along with credit cards and whatnot. And a couple of hundred in his wallet. So it wasn't just a mugger who panicked, at a guess. *Say!*"

"Yes," Shapiro said. "Part of the same problem, Lennie. Pretty unhealthy to work on the *Sentinel,* apparently. Case Cook and I are working on. Not very successfully, I guess. Somebody had a try at him this morning. Missed him, that time."

"Yeah," Richardson said. "We heard at the precinct. Too close to miss him this time, way it looks. Probably sitting right there beside him. Powder burns on his jacket. Left side. Got him right through the heart, way it looks. We've been waiting for the medical examiner's man. But he's sure as hell dead."

Sampson certainly looked dead. He had been sitting near the middle of the bench, the way it looked, with room enough for somebody else to be sitting on it beside him, on his left. Shot, he had fallen to the right, his left foot lifting slightly, his right still dragging on the ground.

He had stopped bleeding. The dead don't bleed. His eyes were still wide open; it seemed to Shapiro that there was still haughtiness in his eyes. Which, of course, was absurd. There is no expression in dead eyes.

"Nobody saw it happen?" Shapiro said.

"Not that we've found. A couple of old-timers were sitting about where those two are—" He gestured toward two elderly men thirty feet or so away on a bench. They were playing checkers. They seemed to be oblivious of what was going on thirty feet away.

"The two other guys were playing checkers too," Richardson said. "Said they didn't see a thing, or hear a thing.

Only thing is, we had to yell at them to make them hear us. Seems both of them were deaf as posts. Gone over to the other side of the park now—where it's quieter, I guess. No dead bodies lying around. Took their checkerboard with them. Thing is, about when it happened, there was a bunch over by the fountain, singing and playing a couple of guitars. Happens most Saturdays and Sundays. They knocked it off when the first patrol car showed up. Came over to see what had happened. We found one of them. Spotted his guitar. He says none of them saw anything or heard anything. Said, 'What the hell, man? We were making music.'"

Sure, he had got the names of some witnesses. Only they were nonwitnesses, or said they were.

About a quarter of two, it had happened. A squeal had come through to precinct at one fifty-four. From somebody who said he had been walking through the park and seen a man lying on a bench and that the man he saw "didn't look right."

"What he told communications, anyway, Nate. Didn't give his name, apparently. They sent a squad car to have a look-see and flashed us. We'd not much more than got here when you two showed up. What we've got is mostly what the men in the patrol cars got. I've got a couple of the boys over at the hotel, on the chance somebody happened to be looking out a window. And Angelo Cartini's trying to find some more of the singing group. Think there'd be somebody who saw something, wouldn't you?"

"Probably there was," Shapiro said. "Somebody who's not sticking his neck out."

People are inclined to avoid involvement. This inclination, which is not confined to New Yorkers, has sometimes resulted in needless deaths. Not, evidently, this time. Leroy Sampson had been dead before anyone's arrival. And where was the assistant medical examiner?

A black sedan, rolling under the arch, answered that. A mortuary van from Bellevue followed it. Neither vehicle was in a special hurry. Their client would wait.

The ambulance men from St. Vincent's put their stretcher, empty, back into their ambulance. One of them flipped a salute toward Lieutenant Richardson. The ambulance pulled away; the sedan pulled in where it had been, and a smallish man with red hair got briskly out of it. He said, "Afternoon, Lennie. So you've got a deader." His speech was as brisk as his movement out of the car had been. He carried the black bag of his trade.

Richardson said, "Yes, Doctor, looks like it."

Dr. Timothy Maloney, assistant medical examiner, County and State of New York, bent over what remained of a man who had been so arrogantly alive an hour or so before. He did not touch the body. He said, "Sure as hell does. Bullet through the heart, at a guess. Aorta, anyway. You finished with it?"

They had finished with it. "All right, boys," Dr. Maloney said to two men who had got out of the van, carrying a rolled canvas stretcher. "All yours."

They took the body of the late Leroy Sampson off the park bench and carried it to the van, limp on the spread-out stretcher. They did put a cloth over the face.

"Let you know soon as we've taken it apart," Maloney said. "And send the slug along. Still in it, way it looks. Stays damned hot for September, doesn't it?"

Richardson agreed it stayed damned hot for September. Dr. Maloney drove off in the small sedan. He drove as briskly as he had moved and spoken. The van followed the car. The van lumbered. "He wouldn't have approved being hustled off like that," Tony Cook said. "From what we saw of him, anyway. People should have been standing at attention. Somebody should have been sounding Taps."

"Yes," Shapiro said, "and maybe we should have given him protection. Offered it, anyway."

"He wouldn't have taken it," Tony said. "He was a cocksure son of a bitch."

Nathan Shapiro merely nodded his agreement. But murdering a son of a bitch remains murder; remains the business of the Homicide Squad, Manhattan South.

"This Enforcer gang?" Tony said.

Nathan Shapiro merely shrugged an answer, which was at the same time a question. Then he said, "Or he saw something, Tony. Could be he was down at the paper yesterday morning. Maybe early yesterday morning. Maybe he saw something then. Maybe he was seen seeing something." He turned to Richardson. "His wife been notified, Lennie?" he said.

"Not that I know of," Richardson said. "What the hell? It just happened. We can call from the squad room, if you know where he lived. Or you can, if you want to."

Nathan Shapiro didn't want to. He never wants to. But often it's part of the job.

"Where'd he live, Tony?" Shapiro said.

Tony had the address of the late Leroy Sampson in his notebook, together with his telephone number. "And his wife's named Emily Louise, Nate. Probably called her Emmy Lou. Want I should give her a ring?"

An escape hatch opened. Shapiro closed it.

"No," he said. "I'll go up there, I think. One of the cruisers can give me a lift. Suppose you stop by and see Mrs. Claye. Maybe she's moved back to Eleventh Street by now. Ask her—oh, whether she's seen Mr. Mead this morning. And whatever else you think of. And then you might see if young Perryman has got home yet. And where he's been since he left us. O.K.?"

Tony said, "Sure."

Sampson's Park Avenue apartment was, from the address, somewhere in the mid-Eighties. Richardson made the arrangements. Shapiro got into the patrol car designated, with two uniformed men in the seat in front of him, and the car rolled toward Fourth Avenue and its journey north. Its absence would leave a gap in the precinct patrol, but the gap would be only temporary. And perhaps no emergency would arise in its absence. Which was, of course, unlikely.

11

The Park Avenue address was a tall apartment building on the northeast corner of Eighty-second Street. The Sampson apartment was on the eighteenth floor. A Negro maid in a white uniform answered Shapiro's ring. She would see if Mrs. Sampson was at home. And who should she say was calling?

Shapiro told her. She looked startled. She would see. If the lieutenant wanted to come in?

Shapiro went into a large entry hall, which was actually part of a much larger living room. The afternoon sun poured into the living room through a window which constituted most of a wall—a south wall, evidently. It was a very expensive living room, part, obviously, of a very expensive apartment. At a guess, it had cost the Sampsons a hundred thousand dollars. No, more likely a hundred and fifty, assuming it was a cooperative apartment building. Nathan Shapiro could only guess as to what the carrying charges were. Even the vaguest of guesses made him wince. Being managing editor of the New York *Sentinel* apparently had been a well-rewarded occupation.

He waited, standing, without going into the bright living room. In spite of the blazing sun, it was comfortably cool in the apartment. He waited some time before a small woman with rippled yellow hair came into the living room. She was younger than he had expected. She had a pretty, rounded face on which life seemed to have left no marks. The face might have been painted on, in watercolor.

The maid followed her into the living room.

As she stepped into the living room, the yellow-haired young woman, who was wearing a dark green robe, put her right hand over her eyes. She said, "What a dreadful glare. *Susie!* Draw the drapes, Susie. How many times do I have to tell you? Everything will get all faded."

Her accent was Southern, her voice high, a little nasal. It was also aggrieved. The maid said, "Yes'm, Mrs. Sampson," and pulled curtains across the big window. The heavy curtains, which Mrs. Sampson thought of as "drapes," darkened the room somewhat.

"And turn on the lamps," said Mrs. Sampson. "Do I have to tell you everything?"

The maid said, "Yes'm, Mrs. Sampson," and touched a switch. Three lamps brightened in the room. Only then did the petite woman appear to become conscious of Nathan Shapiro. She looked at him, and he moved farther into the room.

"You wanted to see me?" Emily Louise Sampson said. Undoubtedly Tony Cook had been right. She was "Emmy Lou." The way she spoke proved it. So, Nathan thought, did her manner. "Susie says you're a policeman of some kind. Of course, they do get things mixed up. You don't look much like a policeman, do you? Policemen wear uniforms."

"Not all of them," Shapiro said. "I'm afraid I have some

bad news for you, Mrs. Sampson. About your husband. Very bad news, I'm afraid."

She opened blue eyes very wide. They remained rather small blue eyes. She put her right hand up to cover her lips. Her mouth, also, was small. It was, however, very exactly contoured.

"My husband couldn't have done anything the police would be interested in," she said. "He couldn't have. It wouldn't be at all like him. He couldn't be mixed up with the police. You must be wrong, you know. Just dreadfully wrong. Mr. Sampson isn't at all the kind of man to get mixed up with the police. What did she say your name was?"

Shapiro told her his name. She said, "Oh," as if much had been explained. Shapiro looked down at her.

"Perhaps you'd better sit down, Mrs. Sampson," he said.

She made no move to sit down. She merely stood and looked at him. She took her fingers down from her lips. There was now, Shapiro thought, a kind of blankness in the smallish blue eyes.

"Mr. Sampson isn't mixed up with the police, Mrs. Sampson. Not in the way you mean. I'm very sorry to have to tell you this. But your husband is dead, Mrs. Sampson. Somebody shot him, I'm afraid."

There is no good way to convey such news. Emily Louise Sampson said, "Oh," drawing it out. Then she said, "Oh, *no.*" She swayed a little, as if he had struck her. But when he started to reach out to steady her, she shrank back away from him. Then she did move a few feet to a deep chair. She sank into it.

Shapiro moved closer, so that he stood in front of the chair, looking down at her. She seemed huddled in the chair. He said, again, how sorry he was to have brought such bad news. Was there somebody who could be with her? Somebody he could call? The maid, perhaps?

At first she did not seem to have heard him. But then

she shook her head. She said, "That stupid little thing? What could she do?"

Shapiro had no answer to that.

"I'll be all right," she said. "Just—oh, just give me a few minutes."

Shapiro said, "Of course." He pulled a light chair up and sat facing her. Then, suddenly, she clenched her hands and began to beat with her fists on both padded arms of the chair. She closed her eyes as she did this. Shock, of course. And angry rejection of what had happened. And, possibly, theatrical demonstration of that shock? He had no special reason to think that.

She had closed her eyes while she pounded at the chair arms. Now she opened them, and put her hands together in her lap. The dark green robe had parted a little as she sank into the chair, but it had not opened too revealingly. Nevertheless, she adjusted it. She looked at Shapiro, her eyes again widely opened. And she said, "Is there something else? Anything else?"

"No, Mrs. Sampson. I thought perhaps you would want to know more about it. About where it happened and how it happened."

"Why should I?" she said. Her voice was high and strained. She sounded, if possible, even more Southern. Leroy Sampson had evidently modified his speech habits more than his wife had when they came out of Alabama.

"Roy's dead, isn't he?" she said. "You say he's dead. That somebody killed him. What more is there?"

Natural curiosity, Shapiro thought. But perhaps it was too soon for that. He said, "I suppose that's all, really. And—well, I'm very sorry, Mrs. Sampson. I hate to have to bring you news like this."

"You say you're a policeman," she said. "I suppose you have to do this sort of thing often. What do you call it? 'Notify survivors.' Isn't that it? And always, I guess, tell them how sorry you are. And then—start asking them questions?"

It was accurate enough. It didn't go very deep; did not indicate any inkling of the inward wrenching such duty brought; any perception that even policemen are human. Still, accurate enough.

"One or two questions, perhaps," he said. "When you feel up to them, of course. Did your husband go down to the Village often, Mrs. Sampson? Greenwich Village, I mean."

She said, "What?" with a note of astonishment in her voice.

Shapiro repeated his question.

"Of course not," she said. "Why ever should he? It's—from what people say, almost as bad as Harlem. All kinds of crazy people down there. Radicals and nigras and that sort of trash. Why would anybody like Roy go to a place like that?"

She was coming out of shock quite rapidly, Shapiro thought, and thought also that Tony Cook would be surprised, and possibly amused, by this description of the Manhattan neighborhood he lived in—had, in fact, been born in. Of course, in recent years, the Negro population of the Village had increased. But not to that extent. The mythology about the Village had, apparently, not diminished, at least in the mind of Emily Louise Sampson.

"I don't know why Mr. Sampson went down to the Village," he said. "On his way home from the office, apparently. We're trying to find out about that. You see, Mrs. Sampson, he was killed there. On a bench in Washington Square. By somebody who was sitting beside him, we think."

"Somebody who was trying to hold him up," she said. "One of those addicts who are all over the place nowadays. Or some nigger—nigra, most likely. They hate white people, you know. They're—well, they're animals really."

Shapiro was tempted to say that we all are, and resisted the temptation. Instead, he said, "We don't think it was just a holdup, Mrs. Sampson. It looks a little as if your husband was shot by someone he knew, was talking to. You don't know anybody he might have gone to meet down there? Somebody who lives in that part of town, say?"

"We don't know anybody like that," she said. "Oh, I think Mr. Perryman's son lives down there someplace. But we don't really *know* him. He works on the paper, Roy told me once. On Roy's staff, actually. But he's just a reporter, I think."

"We know about Mr. Perryman," Shapiro said. "He does live down there, yes. Probably because it's closer to the office. More convenient. Up here, you're quite a way from the *Sentinel* office. And where young Perryman's father lives is almost as far. The older Mr. Perryman is in the hospital now, you know. Somebody shot him, too."

"Roy told me about that," she said. "He—he was very much upset, of course. Mr. Perryman is—"

She stopped suddenly; she leaned forward in the deep chair, and clasped her hands together.

"The way Mr. Claye was," she said, and spoke rapidly, almost convulsively. "And now—now my husband. Is that what you think? What you're getting at?"

"What we're wondering about, yes."

And, he thought, it had taken her some time to make, to wonder about, a rather obvious connection. Still somewhat in shock, apparently. Which was to be expected.

"There was an earlier attempt on your husband's life today, Mrs. Sampson. At the office. Right after he got there. By somebody, we think, who knew when he would get there. Which was always about the same time in the morning, way I get it."

"Always," she said. "There's a cabdriver who always takes him down. Calls up from the lobby every morning. An Eye—Italian, I think he is."

It occurred to Shapiro that Leroy Sampson had married a little beneath him, linguistically, at any rate. Eyetalian. Well, almost. Pretty daughter of what people called a red-neck? Turned into a Southern belle? By her husband? Just when belles, Southern or otherwise, had become an endangered species?

"The night Mr. Claye was killed," Shapiro said. "Thursday night. Early Friday morning, actually. Was your husband home that night?"

"What a strange question," she said. "Surely you can't think my husband had anything—"

"No, Mrs. Sampson. Of course not. But—well, there's an outside chance he might have seen something, heard something, perhaps that would—well, make him dangerous to whoever killed Mr. Claye."

"Some awful Communist," she said. "Surely you can see that. Everybody else does. Roy did. He told me so. Not that I wouldn't have known, anyway. Scum like that. Those dreadful people who paraded in Washington against our boys in Vietnam. When they were just let do it; when nobody stopped them."

Minds wander. Conversations wander too; answers wander away from questions.

"We're not neglecting any possibility, Mrs. Sampson," Shapiro said, sounding to himself as if he were reading from a copybook. "It's quite possible that radical extremists were involved. We realize that. If they were, we'll find them."

"Possible, you say. *Quite* possible. Why, it's *obvious*. Even you must see that."

The "even" which had only been implied before had emerged into the open. "Niggers," of course. Probably also "kikes."

"We're not forgetting that," he told her. "About Thursday night, Mrs. Sampson. Just to keep the record clear. Your husband was here at home Thursday night? And, of course, early Friday morning?"

She couldn't see, couldn't even imagine, what that had to do with the investigation. If he could call it an investigation. And, if he didn't know it, the police commissioner and her husband were—well, had been—friends.

"And," she said, "Mr. Perryman is, too. Or didn't you know that, either?"

"Mr. Perryman mentioned it," Shapiro said. "Commissioner Pierce probably has a good many friends. About Thursday, please. Or if that's something you'd rather not talk about just now—I realize how you must be feeling—well, I can always come back. Or somebody else can, of course. Just to keep the record straight."

"Thursdays have always been Roy's poker nights," she said. "In the fall and winter, anyway. Since we came up here, that is. Out of where we both grew up. Out of where we really belonged, I sometimes think. But my husband would come up here."

"Yes," Shapiro said. "These poker games. They were here, Mrs. Sampson? Or did they sort of rotate around?"

"They were just friendly games, Lieutenant Shapiro. You make them sound—"

Another tangent, another to be blocked off. Shapiro said he realized the poker games were just friendly games, just ways to, once a week, pass evenings. Perhaps he had phrased it badly. The poker players usually met in the Sampson apartment?

"Not since a few years ago," she said. "They used to. But then Roy decided that wasn't fair to me. Men here until all hours. And all the extra work for me. Seeing that they had sandwiches and drinks and things like that. Being a hostess, really. Roy decided three or four years ago not to go on putting me through it. He—he's always been considerate that way, you know."

There was hesitancy in the last statement. When she spoke again, her shrill voice was much lower, almost uncertain. "He was always so good to me," she said. "So careful to see I didn't tire myself out."

Shapiro was sure Mr. Sampson had been a most considerate husband. His tone—he hoped—implied that any man would be of so charming a wife. And after the poker sessions were no longer held in the apartment, they were held somewhere else? At the apartment, or house, or some other man in the group?

"No. They moved them down to the office. There's a big conference room down there—part of the advertising department, I think it is. I've never been there, of course. But that's where I think they go to play. For really quite small stakes. 'Nominal,' he always called them. And only for friends, of course. And not in summer, when so many of us are out of town so much. Or even living in the country, like the Clayes."

Shapiro had not supposed that Leroy Sampson and his associates on the New York *Sentinel* were running a professional gambling establishment, in violation of the laws of the State of New York. His "Of course," to Mrs. Sampson was therefore entirely convincing. Did Mrs. Sampson happen to know who else attended these Thursday night poker sessions? Just as a matter of routine. "They want us to get everything down, you know. Even things which can't possibly matter."

She didn't really know. Mr. Claye was one of them, she thought. Had been for the last year or two. And the advertising manager, whose name she couldn't, for the life of her, remember. Wait a minute. Evans, wasn't it? And Mr. Burns. He was the business manager, she thought.

It came to five, which was enough for a game. Yes, she thought those were the regulars. Sometimes, she had a feeling, a man named Simms, who was "something on the paper." She thought her husband once had mentioned Mr. Simms. Something about Simms having taken "all of us for a cleaning."

That was all the names she could think of. And did it really matter?

"Probably not." And he did appreciate her cooperation, at such a bad time; for her such a sad time. Did she happen to remember whether Mr. Perryman was ever a member of the Thursday night group? She didn't think so; her husband hadn't, that she could remember, mentioned Mr. Perryman as a Thursday night poker player. And Mr. Wainwright? "He's the editor of the *Sentinel,* you know, Mrs. Sampson."

"A very old man," she said. "Should have retired years ago, my husband thought. Yes, I think he was here once or twice when they had the game here. Several years ago, that would have been. I don't know whether he ever played after they moved downtown, where a restaurant could bring them in sandwiches and drinks and things like that."

She had spoken of the games going on until all hours, from which he assumed that Mr. Sampson had often got home late from the poker sessions. Had he, did she remember, been late the previous Friday morning? Yesterday morning?

She hadn't, really, any idea. She herself had gone to bed a little after eleven. Her husband could have got home almost any time after that. He would have been very careful not to awaken her. He was always very careful about that. And, of course, his room was quite a ways from hers. "The other end of the apartment, almost."

She had been very helpful, Shapiro told her, and probably they would not have to bother her again. Except for some formalities, which her attorney could very well handle. And would she be all right alone?

"Oh," she said, "I've got folks down home. They'll come up, of course, when I call them. I won't be alone. I have family."

There was a slight emphasis on the *I.* It was a little as if she alone were so supplied. Shapiro let himself out of the big, glossy apartment.

Managing editors of New York City newspapers were paid handsomely, even when the papers were not particularly profitable.

Or perhaps, of course, Emmy Lou's ancestors had not been red-necks at all. Perhaps they had been wealthy planters, a few generations back possessed of numerous slaves. Perhaps the apartment was her inheritance.

12

Tony Cook was at his desk in the squad room. Motioned to, he followed into Shapiro's office.

David Perryman had gone uptown. "To see a friend and take the friend to lunch," Tony said, "and to tell the friend that their date for a Saturday matinee was off, because he had to be available if his father, still under intensive care at St. Vincent's Hospital, took a turn for the worse. Showed up at the hospital around two, he thinks."

Tony had checked on that. Young Perryman had been admitted to his father's cubicle in the intensive care unit at two ten; he had been allowed five minutes, during which he had done nothing more than sit and look at his unconscious father and watch the zigzag line of the monitor. He had been told that Russel Perryman was holding his own and that it was too soon for a definite prognosis, but that there was cause for hope.

David Perryman, after being assured he would be called if needed, had walked back to his apartment. Since he had been up most of the night before, at the hospital, he had tried to take a nap. Tony Cook's arrival had awakened him.

"Looked it, too," Tony said.

Cook had walked to the Claye house in West Eleventh Street. After a considerable wait, a Japanese in a white jacket had come to the door.

Yes, Mrs. Claye had moved back into the town house; yes, the staff had returned from the country. No, Mrs. Claye was not home at the moment. Well, if it was really important, he could ask Mrs. Claye's personal maid, Marie. If Mr. Cook wanted to wait.

Cook had waited several minutes. He had waited outside, not having been asked in. The Japanese had finally returned. He was sorry he had been so long. He had had to convince Marie that the present whereabouts of Mrs. Roger Claye were any business of the police. He had finally succeeded.

Mrs. Claye had gone uptown, shopping. At about noon. To purchase "suitable clothing." No, Mrs. Claye had not had any visitors during the morning. People had called on the telephone. That was to be expected. Mrs. Claye had answered the telephone herself, for the most part. Two or three calls had been answered first by Marie. No, a call from a Mr. Mead had not been one of those she answered.

And the butler—or houseman—had not let anybody into the house. Yes, he thought he had heard the name Brian Mead. Mrs. Claye had, he thought, mentioned him. He had something to do with the theater. Mrs. Claye was interested in the theater.

It was very sad about Mr. Claye. He had been a most honorable man. And the butler's name was Yoshi, which was short for a much longer name that Mr. and Mrs. Claye had found difficult. And Yoshi was most sorry that Mrs. Claye was out.

"Nothing that helps much," Tony Cook said, and Nathan Shapiro agreed that there wasn't. Mead, if Tony was sure the man who had been finishing a drink at Hugo's bar was Mead, might have been in Greenwich Village for any number of reasons, none of which need concern the police.

Since he was already in that part of town, Tony had gone to the Fifth Avenue Hotel. Its sidewalk café was still open. "Usually is through September, Nate." There was only one couple at a sidewalk table when Tony walked past it into the Fifth Avenue entrance of the hotel.

Tony had got Jason Wainwright's room number and had used the house phone. He had got no answer. The desk clerk had not found Mr. Wainwright's key in the box, but that didn't mean anything. When Mr. Wainwright went out he almost never left his key at the desk. He merely put it in his pocket.

Of course, the Fifth Avenue doorman knew Mr. Wainwright. Mr. Wainwright had lived in the hotel for years. Yes, he had whistled Mr. Wainwright up a cab. A little before noon, he thought it had been. He often got a cab for Mr. Wainwright particularly on Saturday mornings. He had not, of course, ever asked, but he'd somehow got the impression that on Saturdays, Mr. Wainwright usually went uptown for lunch. No, he didn't know where uptown. Once or twice he had heard, or thought he had heard, Mr. Wainwright say, "Gramercy Park," to the cabdriver. But he couldn't be sure. No, that morning he had not heard Mr. Wainwright give any directions. He was helping new guests get their luggage out of a cab while Mr. Wainwright's was pulling away.

A wasted afternoon, as far as Tony Cook was concerned, and as far as he could see. There was, however, one other thing. One of the precinct boys had got a fill-in on last Thursday night's poker game, got it from Ralph Burns, the *Sentinel*'s business manager.

It had been the regular poker game, Burns had told Detective Helms of the precinct squad. Yes, by "regular" he meant that it was held on an agreed night every week, except in summer. Pretty much every week after Labor Day. They played in the conference room of the advertising department. Yes, that was on the fourth floor. It was a large room with comfortable chairs and a suitable table. Mr. Sampson had even arranged to keep one of the elevators running that night, though both of them were usually, Helms was told, shut down nights. "The old man isn't one to waste his money," Burns had said.

There was a nucleus of regular players. Burns himself, Roy Sampson, Evans—Burton Evans, the advertising manager. During the last few years, poor old Claye. As a matter of fact, the game used to be in Sampson's apartment, uptown. Roy had never said so, in so many words, but Burns gathered that Mrs. Sampson, Emily Louise—O.K., Emmy Lou—had got fed up with it. So they'd moved downtown to the Sentinel Building. There was a Canal Street restaurant which would send in sandwiches when ordered. And drinks, sure. But the conference room had its own refrigerator and bar.

Two nights ago? "It was the first game of the fall. If you can call this kind of weather fall. Feels as if we jumped the gun a little. Rounded some players up." Burns himself, Sampson, Claye—"poor guy"—and Evans. A man named Rosen, advertising manager of one of the Fifth Avenue shops, had been expected but had begged off at the last minute. At literally the last minute; at about nine thirty, when they were ready to deal the first hand, with only four players. Rosen was to have been Evans's special guest. "O.K., you could say Burt was buttering him up."

"Four makes a lousy game, you know," Burns had told Detective Helms. "Particularly since Roy always gets himself dealt out a little before eleven, so he can go downstairs and catch the eleven o'clock TV news. Mostly they get their hot stuff from the wire services, way we do, but sometimes one of their own boys comes up with something we need to follow up. Anyhow, Roy Sampson isn't a man to take chances."

It was then that Detective Helms had explained that Leroy Sampson was no longer to be spoken of in the present tense. Burns had said, "Jesus Christ!" and had asked what the hell was going on around here? Helms told him that was what they were trying to find out. And had they tried to rustle up a fifth for the game?

After announcing that he'd be damned, he sure as hell would, Burns had said that they had tried to ring in old Wainwright, who'd been pretty much a regular a few years back and had dropped out. "Getting along, old Jase is. Not up to much nowadays. Keeps getting physical checkups. Used to be quite a poker player."

Somebody, Claye as he remembered it, had called Jason Wainwright at the Fifth Avenue Hotel. Wainwright had said he'd like to, but didn't feel up to it. "Hell, he must be damned near eighty."

So the four of them had played. One hand of draw, as Burns remembered it, and one of five-card stud. "I won a couple of dollars at draw. With a pair of nines, for God's sake. Lost them at stud, with a third king in the hole for Roy. And that time, I had a pair of aces. Goes to show, doesn't it?"

Helms agreed that it went to show. He said, "A couple of dollars, Mr. Burns?"

"Oh," Burns said, "I didn't mean that literally. More like maybe fifty. But we don't play for high stakes. On the other hand, it isn't precisely penny ante."

The stud hand had taken some time, partly because of Burns's mistaken confidence in his pair of aces. It had been about twenty of eleven when Sampson had raked in his chips and stacked them and looked at his watch. And asked to be dealt out while he went down to listen to "those elitist bastards on CBS." He had gone down. Yes, Burns supposed, by elevator. And did Helms know how the old boy was making out?

The last Helms had heard, Russel Perryman was still in intensive care at St. Vincent's; still on the critical list. And about how long had Mr. Sampson been away from the game?

"Until about, oh, eleven thirty, at a guess. We knocked it off and had a round of drinks. Three isn't any kind of a game, you know."

Helms agreed that three-handed poker isn't much of a game, although perhaps preferable to three-handed bridge. So Mr. Sampson had come back about half-past eleven, and the four of them had continued playing. "Until around when, Mr. Burns?"

Only until around midnight, as Burns remembered it. Then Roger Claye said he'd have to sign off; that he had a little work to do. No, he had not said what the work was. "I assumed he'd thought of something he wanted to get into his column. His Friday column. Something he'd just thought of, maybe."

Claye had left the advertising department's conference room, or gambling room. Burns had assumed he was going home, or, if the house was still closed up, back to his hotel. "Seems he didn't," Burns said. "Seems he went downstairs to that office of his."

"Way it looks," Helms said. "None of you got the idea he was going somewhere to meet somebody?"

Burns had not. He had supposed that Claye, as Claye had said, had some work to do. Presumably on his column for the following day. Neither Evans nor Sampson had expressed any doubts, or raised any question, about Roger Claye's intentions. "Nobody thought he was going off to get himself killed." If that was what Helms was getting at.

"Well," Helms said, "he did meet somebody. He did get himself killed. The rest of you—you and Mr. Sampson and Mr. Evans. You go on playing?"

They had not. They had had a final drink. Then Sampson had left. Yes, he and Evans had gone down together in the same elevator. Sampson was not around. "Probably had his usual taxi waiting. He's got—used to have—a tame driver. Before that, he had his own car and a chauffeur, for God's sake. Way I get it, Emmy Lou's got it coming out of her ears. Father was in textiles or something. In a big way, at a guess. Or maybe Wallace gave him liquor distributing rights, or something. Anyway, Mrs. Sampson's rolling in the stuff. Rolling alone now, apparently. Makes you think, doesn't it?"

Helms had admitted it made a person think.

"Didn't say what about," Tony Cook said, finishing a rather long narrative to Lieutenant Nathan Shapiro. "Anyway, they all managed to get taxis. Evans lives on lower Fifth somewhere. Burns has an apartment in the East Sixties—I've got their addresses, if we want them."

"This Helms seems to have known the questions to ask, doesn't he?" Nathan said. "Sampson was away from the game for more than half an hour, apparently. Plenty of time for him to have seen something. If there was anything to see, of course."

"Yes," Tony said. "Or some*body*."

Nathan Shapiro nodded his agreement. It was what he had had in mind. He looked sadly down at his desk. There were papers on it. There were always papers on it.

One of the papers he looked at, discouragement on his face, was a report from the lab, from the experts who had been comparing typing from various machines in the *Sentinel* offices. Comparisons had so far got them nowhere in particular. Oh, the letter from something calling itself "The Enforcers" to Edmond Riley, city editor, had been typed on an Underwood. No idiosyncrasies had been found in the typefaces. To be sure, the *e* was slightly out of line, microscopically out of line. None of the comparison copies showed this misalignment, which was, in any case, too slight to be of much use, particularly in court—when it comes to court. If it comes to court.

The Enforcers' typewriter had been manually operated,

not an electric. Whoever had used it had had a heavy touch. The periods had punched holes in the paper, which was Eagle Trojan Bond, sub. 20—in common enough use.

Nothing helpful. Shapiro had not supposed there would be.

Headquarters had no record of a terrorist organization which called itself "The Enforcers." Or of a crackpot group of any kind so called. Which didn't, of course, prove anything. Or proved merely that The Enforcers had not previously surfaced.

So there we are, Shapiro thought. Nowhere in particular. He looked across his desk at Detective Anthony Cook. "Yeah," Cook said, "some guys playing poker. Two floors above where Claye got hit. And a twenty-two doesn't make a noise like a cannon."

Shapiro made no response to this and Tony Cook had expected none. Cook had merely spoken to establish his continued presence. He doubted he had. Nathan continued to look through him, apparently at the wall beyond.

Then, as much to the wall as to Tony, Shapiro said, "A man approaching eighty does get concerned about his health, of course. Sees that he has regular checkups. Maybe—"

He did not amplify the "Maybe." Instead, he said, "We've got Mr. Simms's telephone number, Tony? His home number? Although probably, nice afternoon like this, he'll be out somewhere."

It was late afternoon; it was after five. Their shift had been over for more than an hour. Tony had a date, but it was not until seven. Rose, long used to her role as a policeman's wife, wouldn't start to wonder until well after six. It would be later when she would start to worry.

Tony had the telephone number of Peter Simms. Shapiro got an outside line and dialed it. It took Simms only three rings to answer. Shapiro was sorry to keep bothering him.

It was no bother. Simms had just started to mix their

evening cocktails. Anything he could do to help, and it was a damn shame about Sampson. There was, however, no note of deep grief in Simms's voice. To Shapiro's next question there was a moderately surprised "Huh?"

No, if Jason Wainwright was worried about his health he had kept his worries to himself.

"Last guy in the world to bore people with his symptoms, Jase is," Simms said. "Get to be his age, you're pretty sure to have them, I suppose. But you'd never catch Jase whining about them, way some people do. Take my esteemed —no, don't take her. Take anybody in his late seventies, I suppose. But not Wainwright."

"Happen to know, Mr. Simms, whether Mr. Wainwright had regular physical checkups? Mr. Burns seems to think he did."

"Never mentioned them to me," Simms said. "Could be he did to Burns. But Burns is a worrier himself. Hears about something and right away is sure he has it. And rushes off to his doctor. His most recent doctor. Probably has the idea everybody does the same. Why this sudden interest in Wainwright's health, Lieutenant?"

"Just routine. Nothing special. As far as you know, he's in good health? For a man his age, anyway?"

"Sure. Come to think of it, he did say something about it a month or so back. He'd been to a hospital for a thorough going-over, and had been away from the office for about a week. When he came back, he said he'd been sorry to dump everything on me and that they'd given him a clear bill. Said one of the doctors told him, 'You'll probably outlive all of us.' Tickled the old boy, because the doctor looked like being somewhere in his fifties."

No, Simms did not know to what hospital Wainwright had gone for his checkup. Could be St. Vincent's, which wasn't too far from the hotel Wainwright lived in. But he didn't know. If he had ever known, he'd forgotten. Then, unexpectedly, "Damn!"

He left it there, while Shapiro waited.

"Nothing," Simms said. "I was mixing our drinks when the phone rang. Can't remember whether I put the vermouth in. Have to assume I did, I guess. Better none than too much. Right?"

Shapiro did not answer that, having no idea what the right answer would be. He again apologized for bothering the associate editor of the New York *Sentinel,* whose name, unlike that of the paper's city editor, did appear on the masthead.

He got from Tony Cook the telephone number of the Claye town house. He dialed it.

The response this time was not so quick. It was after the fourth ring, midway of the fifth, that a man said, "The Claye residence." Lieutenant Shapiro? If the lieutenant would wait, please? Shapiro waited. The next voice was female. "Ullo? This is Marie. I will see whether Madame is free."

"Yes, Lieutenant?" On a note of extreme, if tried, patience. "Yes, this is Faith Claye. Are there more questions? It has been a very—trying day. As perhaps you can realize, Lieutenant Shapiro."

The "even you" was implied in the markedly New England voice.

"Just one thing we've been wondering about," Shapiro told her. "Your husband's state of mind the last few weeks."

"State of mind, Lieutenant? What an odd question. What do you mean, precisely?"

"Well, say, was he in good spirits? Cheerful? Or, possibly, apprehensive? As if he were disturbed about something? Anything you can tell us about his state of mind?"

She did not see how that would help anyone in any way. And she was quite tired, as perhaps he could appreciate. In any case, her husband had seemed, recently, much as he always was. Certainly not "apprehensive," whatever the lieutenant might have in mind by that. He was never what could be called apprehensive, if Lieutenant Shapiro meant about himself. Did he think her husband had been afraid someone would kill him? No more than anybody else, the way things had got to be in this country.

"The only thing Roger was apprehensive about was the country's drift," Faith Claye said. "Drift into socialism, into a kind of welfare state, with people who won't work, living on —sponging on—people who do work. Who have the work ethic which is dying out. And those awful unions, which are strangling the free enterprise system. And the government's determination to run all our lives. About things like that, of course he was what you call apprehensive. Never about himself. My husband was a brave man, Lieutenant Shapiro. A fighter. If you understand what I mean."

Shapiro did understand what she meant. He was sure Roger Claye had been brave, and a courageous fighter against the welfare state. Against the burgeoning relief rolls. And against free lunches for schoolchildren from impoverished—and therefore, of course, shiftless—families. He managed, he hoped, to convey all this in the tone of his "Yes, Mrs. Claye. We're sure he was." And Mr. Claye had seemed in good spirits the last few weeks? (Except, of course, about the dangerous drift of the country from the spirit of its founders. And, as went without saying, the free enterprise system. Since it went without saying, Shapiro did not say it.)

Mr. Claye was always in good spirits, in spite of everything. During the last week or so of his life, although really she had not seen much of him, he had seemed in even better spirits than usual. Perhaps because he had had great hopes for Governor Reagan. "He thought Reagan was the hope of the country."

Shapiro saw what she meant and was sure that Mr. Claye had been a very patriotic man. Would she go so far as to say that recently her husband had seemed elated, set up about something? The possible salvation of the country from its downward plunge? (Which had, of course, started with Franklin Roosevelt.)

Elated was perhaps too strong a term. He had seemed—well, more hopeful than he usually was. About things in general, perhaps. And he had, she thought, been pleased with his recent columns. "He wasn't always. Sometimes he felt he wasn't hitting hard enough. Wasn't really getting his point across. He got that way sometimes. A little that way. But I think Mr. Perryman said something recently that—well, reassured him. He didn't tell me that, of course. But I felt that something like that had happened. My husband and I were really very close, Lieutenant. We didn't need to spell things out to each other."

Shapiro said he completely understood, and that he was very sorry to have had to bother her so much at a time like this.

She said she appreciated that and, if there was nothing else, she thought she would go and lie down a while.

Shapiro said, "Yes, do that, Mrs. Claye. We'll try not to bother you again."

He hung up.

13

ROGER CLAYE had had no premonition of violent death. He had been, in recent days, in good spirits, if elated was too strong a word. Russel Perryman, owner and publisher, had recently said something to him which increased his usually sanguine mood. (Except, of course, about the nation's "drift." Away from the principles advocated by Ronald Reagan and, presumably, George Wallace.)

Which, of course, got them nowhere. Nothing much did; Shapiro's day, like Mrs. Claye's, had been "trying." The mind gets fagged out at the end of such a day. Perhaps things would come clearer on another day. Shapiro rather doubted it, but there was always a chance. All right, an outside chance. All chances in an alien land are outside chances.

Perhaps tomorrow, Russel Perryman, publisher and owner, would recover sufficiently to tell them who had shot him from the dimness of an elevator car he had been about to walk into. Perhaps tomorrow they would merely have to find somebody, and assure him he had a right to remain silent and put handcuffs on him—and try to persuade him not to remain silent.

Nathan Shapiro pushed his chair back from his desk and started to stand up. He said, "I guess, Tony, we may as well call it—" and the telephone bell interrupted him. He said "Shapiro" into it and sat down again. He motioned to Tony Cook, and Cook sat down. Shapiro said, "Go ahead, Strom," to Detective Wilfred Strom, of Homicide South, who had spent an extremely dull afternoon in a corner of the small private room allotted Russel Perryman in the intensive care unit at St. Vincent's Hospital. A uniformed patrolman had spent an equally boring afternoon outside the door of Perryman's room. But the uniformed man had been able to smoke, if he wanted to smoke, as long as he made sure that nobody but nurses and doctors went into the room.

"He said *what?*" Shapiro said to Detective Strom. "About *football!*"

Perryman had partly regained consciousness, partly and briefly. He had muttered something and Strom, allowed to lean over the bed and listen, had made out a little of the muttering. And, yes, Perryman had seemed to be muttering about football. He had, Strom thought, said "team," and said it several times. Once, as nearly as Strom could make out, he had said, "My team," and again, "Not on it," and something that sounded like "Dragging feet."

"It was pretty hard to make out what he *was* trying to say, Lieutenant," Strom said. "He could just whisper, and even that came out sort of—well, mushy. The nurse was listening, too, and couldn't get it any clearer than I could. Only she thought that once he said something like 'quarterback,' which was what made me think of football. Only it didn't sound much like that to me. Anyway, then he closed his eyes and seemed to go back to sleep and the nurse made me go back to the corner I'd been sitting in."

"That's all, Strom?"

"I know it's not much, Lieutenant. Not anything, I guess. But the captain told me anything, anything at all, I was to call in."

"Yes, Strom," Shapiro said. "Anything at all. You getting any idea how they think he's making out?"

"They don't seem to know, sir. The nurse who was there seemed to think it was encouraging he came out of it at all. Said now it seemed more like sleep than coma. But then she got one of the doctors and then, they shooed me out. They don't much like my being in the room at all, you know. I'm outside now. It just happened."

"Go back in when they'll let you, Strom. I'll try to get you a relief in an hour or so. Anybody tried to get in to see Mr. Perryman?"

"Not really. His son's standing by. Out in the waiting room. And a man named Wainwright—something like that—came around to see Perryman, but they said no visitors and he went away again. I got that from the man outside—the precinct man."

"This Mr. Wainwright. He wasn't insistent on getting in? Didn't make any pitch about it?"

"Not from what I heard. Just said he understood and when Perryman came out of it to tell him Wainwright had called. The doctor's just come out, Lieutenant, and Evelyn, she's the nurse, is motioning I can go back in."

Shapiro told him to go back in, and again promised him relief as soon as possible. He hung up and told Tony Cook what Strom had reported. Tony said it seemed like a hell of a time for Perryman to be worrying about football.

"Everybody, from the President down, seems to be talking in football terms nowadays," Shapiro said. "About 'members of my team.' That sort of thing. I wonder if Perryman was—"

He did not finish, but merely looked at Tony Cook.

"Yeah," Tony said. "So do I, I guess. Maybe Perryman didn't really mean quarterback."

Shapiro nodded his head.

"And it could be," Shapiro said, "Perryman thought he was talking to somebody. Repeating what he had said to somebody. Or, could be, going over in his mind—sort of rehearsing—what he was going to say to somebody. Could have been that, couldn't it, Tony?"

Tony agreed that it could have been that. Nathan regarded the wall beyond Tony Cook, and what he saw there seemed to distress him. But it also seemed to Tony that Shapiro's distress was—well, more concentrated. It was an expression he had seen before, often seen before, on Shapiro's long, sad face. It had meant before that Nathan Shapiro was beginning to see, or to hope he was beginning to see, a shape to things. Which might mean they were nearing the end of it.

Which also probably meant that Tony would have to telephone Rachel Farmer and tell her it wouldn't be seven o'clock but some time after that. If at all. Well, he was a cop by choice. And if he weren't a cop, he probably wouldn't have met Rachel at all. She had, after all, been a suspect when he had first met her and had seemed angular, as well as tall. One lived and learned.

Nathan Shapiro used the telephone. He dialed for an outside line. Then he dialed on it. Tony could hear the crackle of an answer, and the answer was in a female voice.

"Yes, dear, I'm afraid so," Shapiro said. "Yes again. Yes, as usual. Yes, Rose, as soon as I possibly can. I'm sorry too. Unless it's too urgent, I'll walk her when I get home. When I can, dear."

He hung up. He also stood up. Tony was already on his feet. Tony said, "Where?"

"The hospital," Shapiro said, and his tone added, "Of course." It wasn't that clear to Tony Cook, but he said, "O.K., sir."

"To have a word with the kid," Nathan said, explaining things fully. "See if you can get us a car, huh?"

Tony got them a squad car. The car, with Tony driving, took them across and downtown to St. Vincent's hospital. An elevator took them up to the floor of the intensive care unit. They walked past a door marked, "Intensive Care. No Visitors." There was a small waiting room a little way down the corridor. David Perryman was alone in it. He was smoking a cigarette, and there was an almost empty paper cup of coffee on the floor beside his chair. He was wearing a dark blue sports shirt, open at the neck, and a lighter blue sports jacket. He stood up when they went into the room and looked at them. There was anxiety in his young face.

"All right, son," Shapiro said. "No bad news. Actually, your father regained consciousness for a few minutes a while back. Encouraged his doctors, I understand. My name is Shapiro, by the way. Detective Cook you've met. There are just a couple of things we'd like to clear up."

Young Perryman said, "Sure," and sat down again. He took a final drag at his cigarette and stubbed it out. Shapiro pulled a chair nearer and sat on it. It was not a very comfortable chair; St. Vincent's did not encourage their visitors to linger unduly.

"We have to consider all possibilities," Shapiro said. "Your father'll probably be all right, they tell us. But if he shouldn't recover, I suppose you inherit his estate? Including the *Sentinel?*"

"I suppose so," David Perryman said. "I don't know of anybody else, now that Mother's dead. I've never thought about it much. Father's always seemed—well, I've never thought about his dying."

"Probably he'll be all right," Shapiro said. "Laid up for a while, of course. Not be able to be very active in running the paper. In that case, you'd have to take over, I suppose?"

"No. Oh, they'd check with me, I suppose. Keep me

filled in, you know. But Mr. Wainwright would be in charge. He and Sampson, I guess. And Mr. Burns, of course."

"Not Sampson," Shapiro told him. "I take it you haven't heard. Mr. Sampson is dead. Somebody shot him. Early this afternoon."

Perryman said, "*Jeeze!*" There appeared to be complete surprise in the expletive. Then he said, "What the hell is going on, Mr. Shapiro?"

"Lieutenant," Shapiro said. "We're trying to find out."

"When did this happen?" Perryman said. "To Mr. Sampson, I mean."

"Around two this afternoon. A little before or after. In Washington Square."

"I was at the hospital then," Perryman said. "Or on my way there. As I told Detective Cook this"—he looked at Tony—"it *was* just this afternoon, wasn't it? Did you check on it?"

"We checked," Shapiro said. "If the worst comes to the worst, Mr. Perryman—if your father doesn't make it—what'll you do about the *Sentinel*? Sell it?"

"I don't know, really. To be honest, it might be hard to find a buyer. It's—well, not so profitable as it used to be. Everybody knows that, I guess. Some of the big advertisers have—well, got sore at us for some reason. Others have just sort of drifted away."

"Any idea why this has happened? This drifting away, I mean?"

"It's a bad time for afternoon papers in this town. Anybody will tell you that. Used to be, oh, half a dozen. Now just two, the *Post* and us. And the *Post* has had to change a lot, since the days Curtis owned it. A long ways before my time, that was. People moving to the suburbs, I guess. And the big stores moving there after them. Take Wanamaker's, for instance. Used to buy the whole back page of the New York *Sun* every day, when there was a New York *Sun*. And, come to that, a New York Wanamaker's."

"Just a change in the times, Mr. Perryman? A shift in population? What they call a flight from the inner city?"

"What Dad thinks. Says he thinks, anyway."

"Nothing about the paper itself? Its policies, say?"

David Perryman hesitated. He hesitated long enough to light another cigarette. Then he said, "Well," drawing it out. "Mr. Wainwright thinks that enters into it," he said then. "Not that he doesn't agree with the policy. I think he does. But he thinks we're too violent. Too one-sided. Not really a newspaper any more. Just—well, he says, a propaganda sheet. Once he said the *Sentinel* was becoming a house organ, and that nobody trusted it any more. He's pretty extreme about it, but I think maybe he's right—partly right, I mean."

"You've talked to Mr. Wainwright about this? About the way he feels?"

"Some. The last year or so we've got sort of friendly. Considering how old he is, I mean. I've even had dinner with him over at the hotel he's lived in since his wife died. I don't know why he wants to be friendly with me. I must seem like a kid to him. A small boy, almost. Hell, Mr. Wainwright must be damned near eighty."

There was a kind of disbelief in his voice when he spoke of Wainwright's being near eighty. Eighty was, his tone said, an unthinkable age.

"He talked to you as if you were a kid?"

"Funny thing is, it didn't feel that way. More like one man to another. Maybe one newspaperman to another. He's kind of hipped on newspapers. On being a newspaperman."

"You're not, I take it?"

"Not the way Mr. Wainwright is. Oh, it sort of grows on you. There's something about writing a hot story for an edition. Rushing it along, if you know what I mean. And getting a good story to write, maybe the lead story sometimes. It's, well, pretty exciting. And feeling you're getting pretty good at it. All right at it, anyway. That you're really learning your trade. Exciting, I guess you'd say. Probably sounds pretty silly to you, Lieutenant."

"No," Shapiro said. "I can see how anyone would feel excited knowing he was getting good at something. Anyone could feel that way, I'd think. Sense of accomplishment, I suppose you'd call it. You feel that way about your work on the *Sentinel?*"

"Beginning to, anyway. Get a good story nowadays, Riley lets me go on with it. While back, he'd take it away from me and give it to Fremont, or one of the others. Or not give it to me in the first place, if it looked like it might be big. The last year or so, Riley's acted like he's beginning to trust me. O.K.—it's sort of encouraging. I'm not just my father's son any more. Just an all-right member of the city staff."

"Yes," Shapiro said. "And now, perhaps, you're beginning to feel that you're turning into a real newspaperman. Like Mr. Wainwright, maybe."

"Hell, no. I've been on the paper two or three years. He's been on it, I guess, maybe fifty."

"Was it about the time you began to feel Mr. Riley was trusting you that you began to see a good deal of Mr. Wainwright?"

"I guess so."

"Did he institute this friendship, would you say?"

"I suppose so. A cub reporter doesn't move in on the editor of a paper. I don't suppose, Lieutenant, you go around slapping the commissioner on the back. Saying, 'Howdy, pal?'"

Nathan Shapiro, who never slaps anybody on the back, smiled and said, "No, son." Then he said, "If you have to run the paper while your father is convalescing—or if he dies—will you make any changes in the way it's run? Give Mr. Wainwright more authority, perhaps? Change the way the news is handled in any way?"

"I don't know," Perryman said. "Maybe. Gradually.

What's this all about, Lieutenant Shapiro? What's it got to do with what you're working on?"

"We're just fumbling around," Shapiro told him. "Trying to get the whole picture. You'd have to get a new managing editor, obviously. Who'd it be, Mr. Perryman?"

"That's easy," Perryman said. "Ed Riley, of course. He's damn good. And he's not a—"

He stopped with that. He would not, Shapiro suspected, have used a word which would have been admiring of the late Leroy Sampson. "Bigot," perhaps. Or "slave driver?" He did not press the point.

"About Mr. Wainwright," he said. "Would you give him more authority?"

"If he wanted it," Perryman said. "I don't think he would. He said to me once that he was just staying around to keep an eye on things. Way he put it. As I said, he's damn near eighty. Not that it's affected his mind, far as I can see."

"Mr. Sampson thought Mr. Wainwright is wishy-washy. Way he put it. You don't think that, I gather?"

"Hell, no. Sampson thought anybody was that who didn't agree with him, agree violently. Probably thought Mr. Wainwright was, like they used to say, 'soft on communism.' Because he didn't scream about it all the time. Probably thought I am, too. Told Ed Riley once not to give me any stories with a political slant. Told him I couldn't be trusted not to let my own prejudices creep in. *Jesus! My* prejudices. For Sampson, if you voted the Democratic ticket—except for Wallace—you were a scoundrel. Probably a traitor to boot. And he saw to it that that belief showed up in the news stories. And, for God's sake, in the way the desk edited AP stories. If you can believe that."

"That's a bad thing to do?" Shapiro said, asking out of ignorance. Tony had heard, at Perryman's apartment yesterday, of the editing of AP stories. Apparently, to a newspaperman, a real crime.

"Unless it's just for length," Perryman was saying, "it's a

violation of the franchise. We could lose ours, if they wanted to be tough about it."

Shapiro said he saw, which was something of an exaggeration.

"If Mr. Wainwright should retire," he said, "who would you put in his place, if you were running things? Mr. Simms?"

"Probably. If he wanted it. Rumor going around, though, he's had an offer from the *Chronicle*. Probably take it."

He stubbed out the cigarette he had just lighted.

"I don't get this," David Perryman said, and there was a hint of shrillness in his voice. "First you tell me the doctors are encouraged about Dad. Then you go into all this business about what I'll do if he dies. Were you just kidding me along at first? Is Dad really—"

He was interrupted. A nurse came into the small waiting room. She wore a very white uniform and a very nursely smile. She directed the smile at Perryman. She said, "You still here, Mr. Perryman? Because you can go home safely at any time. Your father is resting comfortably now, and the doctors are much encouraged. And tomorrow they hope he can be taken out of intensive care to his own room. Isn't that good news, Mr. Perryman?"

"Yes, nurse," Perryman said. "Very good news. Can I see him?"

The nurse retained her smile, but she shook her head.

"He's sleeping now," she said. "It's the best thing for him, we think. Tomorrow, Mr. Perryman. Probably tomorrow, after he's had a good night's rest. And you look as if you could use a night's rest yourself. You were here most of last night, they tell me. We don't want you to become a patient too, do we?"

There was solicitude in her voice. Shapiro thought it was professional, but made no comment. He stood up.

"We're really getting along very nicely," the nurse said, and went out of the room.

David Perryman had stood when the nurse came into the room. Now he looked at Shapiro and waited.

"Of course, Mr. Perryman," Shapiro said. "Go home and get some rest, as the nurse says. If there's anything more, we'll be in touch. I don't think there will be. You've been very helpful."

Young Perryman shrugged his shoulders.

"I don't see how," he said. But he went out of the waiting room.

Tony Cook wasn't sure he saw how either. Or maybe he did. In a muffled sort of way.

"I think we'd better take a little ride downtown, Tony," Shapiro said, and there was a lift in his voice. Or Tony thought there was. They went down to the car. They had parked in a no parking zone, but there was no slip under the wiper. And the car hadn't been towed away, although there was nothing to indicate it was a police car. Getting sloppy, the traffic boys were. Or shorthanded, as the city's economy required.

And, in Tony's opinion, which had not been asked or was likely to be, a hell of a lot too many men chasing small-time gamblers and picking up prostitutes, enforcing a moral code which had no real connection with the city's safety. Which was merely in accord with laws mistakenly on the books.

He drove the squad car south on Seventh Avenue, assuming what Nate had meant by "downtown." Shapiro said nothing to dispel this assumption. He parked on Broadway in front of the Sentinel Building.

The main entrance door was closed, but not locked. The big lobby was dim, except for light coming through the door of the pharmacy-lunch counter at the far end. There was a much dimmer light behind the closed doors marked "The New York Sentinel. Business Office." There was no guard in the lobby. Both elevators were at the ground floor, with their doors open but no light on inside them.

Shapiro and Cook went up the stairs beside the elevators. A low-watt bulb lighted the stairs dimly.

They went through the city room, which was deserted, and into the corridor leading toward the private offices. The ticker room was lighted, and the tickers were clattering already, although it was not yet seven o'clock, piling the floor with wide ribbons of paper, with what was going on in the world typed on them. At the moment, nobody on the *Sentinel* staff was paying attention. It was Saturday night; the *Sentinel* was somnolent for the weekend.

They stopped in front of the closed door to what had been the office of Leroy Sampson, managing editor. Looking down the passageway between office doors to its far end, they looked at two more doors, both also closed—doors to the offices of Jason Wainwright, editor, and Peter Simms, his associate.

"Tell you what, Tony, suppose you get samples from their typewriters. Just to give the lab boys something to play around with."

"O.K.," Tony said. "Assuming I can get in. Wainwright keeps his locked, way I got it."

"But I doubt Simms does," Shapiro told him. "And there's a door between the offices, way I remember it. And, after all, you've got your gimmick, Tony."

The police have a gimmick for obstinate locks. They are not, of course, supposed to use it, except in emergencies.

Tony said "O.K." again and walked down toward the offices. Shapiro stood and watched him. He watched Tony Cook try the door of Wainwright's office. Evidently it was locked. He went to Simms's which, just as evidently, was not. He opened it and turned on a light inside and closed it after him. There was a streak of light visible under the door.

Shapiro kept on waiting for several minutes. Cook would be typing the injunction to all good men. Or perhaps the one concerning the activities of the quick brown fox. It was taking him a little longer than Shapiro would have expected.

Then the thin streak of light appeared under the door to Wainwright's office, as Shapiro had supposed it would. Shapiro nodded, to nobody in particular and quite without realizing he had done so.

The light under Wainwright's door vanished. So, seconds later, did the light under Simms's door. Tony Cook came back up the corridor, carrying copy paper folded in his left hand.

"You were right about the connecting door," Tony said. "And it wasn't locked. And Wainwright's typewriter is an electric, which the lab boys say it wasn't."

Which was clear enough to Nathan Shapiro, who said, "We may as well send them both along, anyway. Let the lab boys earn their salaries."

They went back through the empty city room and back down the dimly lighted stairs. In the car, Shapiro said they might as well find telephones and then get a bite to eat. He suggested that both might be available at, say, the Fifth Avenue Hotel.

Tony felt he had missed a beat, but he was not really surprised.

14

WEST NINTH STREET in Manhattan is a one-way street. It is also a bus street. Parking on the north side of the street between Fifth and Sixth is forbidden at all times. This rule is not too strictly adhered to, although it is enforced if a cruise car happens to be passing through the block. So when Tony parked the squad car a little beyond the Ninth Street entrance to the Fifth Avenue Hotel, which does not have a doorman in attendance, he flicked up a sign behind the windshield. The sign had N Y P D printed on it in large letters. It was, after all, a tow-away zone, and a cruising cop might well miss the identifying numbers on the license plate.

In the big lobby, they found telephone booths, and each went into one and each dialed a familiar number.

Rose Shapiro was resigned; she had expected no better. She has been a policeman's wife for a good many years. All right, she wouldn't expect him for dinner. She would expect him when she saw him. Yes, she would walk Cleo. Of course, she would walk her on only the main, and well-lighted, street. "And you be careful too, Nathan."

Rachel Farmer's association with a policeman has not been so long, but she is learning. She did say, "Damn it, Tony. Not again!" She added that he was always standing her up, and that if he was later than, say, ten, he would probably find her asleep because, after all, she was a working woman and had an appointment tomorrow. Yes, even if tomorrow was Sunday. All right, Simonsky was a Sunday painter. Also, he could afford to pay a model twice the usual fee for Sunday work.

Rachel's work as a model is usually dull and almost always exhausting. But it pays well.

After Shapiro had told Rose that, as always, he was sorry and to be sure not to walk Cleo in any dark places, he looked up the telephone number of St. Vincent's Hospital and dialed it. He identified himself to the nurses' station on the intensive care floor, and was assured that Mr. Perryman was resting comfortably and that his condition was considered stabilized. Yes, the lieutenant could be switched to Records.

He had to wait some time for Records to come on. Hospitals reduce their clerical staffs on weekends. When it answered, Records was female and doubtful. Was Lieutenant Shapiro sure he was Lieutenant Shapiro? And did he know that it was after seven on a Saturday evening and that clerical staffs, even at hospitals, rate reasonably decent hours? Well, if it was important, she'd check.

There was then a considerable period of silence, broken now and then by the sound of file drawers being closed with evident energy. Then—

Yes, Mr. Jason Wainwright had been an inpatient about a month ago—from August tenth to August fifteenth. For a variety of tests, including numerous X rays. The tests were under the direction of Dr. James Hamilton, an internist. No, not an intern, for heaven's sake. A specialist in internal medicine. Yes, she could say that the tests seemed to have been quite comprehensive. Was there anything else?

There was, of course, but Shapiro merely said, "No. Just checking up a little. Thank you," and hung up. Records would not tell him the outcome of the comprehensive tests, even if Records knew it.

Tony Cook was on a house telephone when Nathan came out of the booth. He cradled the phone and said, "No soap. Doesn't answer. Probably having dinner somewhere."

"Probably," Shapiro said. "You ever eat here, Tony?"

Tony had, but not for several years. The food had been all right, and they didn't stick you too hard for it. He had a feeling that, a few years back, the restaurant had been a concession, and that somebody else was running it now. The hotel management itself, maybe.

"We may as well try it," Shapiro said. "Now that we're here."

"Or," Tony said, "we could have him paged and, if he doesn't show, go over to Hugo's."

Shapiro shook his head to that.

The main restaurant at the Fifth Avenue Hotel opens off the lobby. It is large and, looked into through glass-paneled doors, seemed to be largely populated. A party of some sort, evidently, with some of the men in dinner jackets. And a good many couples dancing to the music of a small combo.

"There's the bar," Tony said. "They serve in there. Used to, anyway."

The barroom was on the Fifth Avenue side of the hotel. The bar itself ran along one wall, and there were two barmen behind it and half a dozen men and two women on stools in front of it. There were some twenty tables in the room, six of them by windows giving on the now dusky Fifth Avenue.

Most of the tables were occupied. A man in a dinner jacket said, "Two, gentlemen?" and looked around the room.

He said it might be a few minutes, and if they would care to wait at the bar?

They went to the bar and got stools side by side. The barman nearest said, "Gentlemen?" Shapiro said, "A glass of sherry, please," and spoke sadly, being sure the sherry would be what they called "dry" and hence barely drinkable. Tony ordered a dry martini. He put emphasis—undue emphasis, Nathan thought—on the word "dry."

The barman turned away. He scooped shaved ice out of a bin under the bar and filled a cocktail glass with it. Then he filled a taller, narrow wineglass.

Tony spoke, using a low voice. "Window table, third down," Tony said.

"Yes," Shapiro said. "Saw him as we came in. Didn't see us, I think. Just looking out the window."

They could see the sidewalk café out the window. There was a young couple at one of the sidewalk tables. They were drinking coffee. Their heads were rather close together. And people were walking beyond the café—a tall black man, and a much shorter—and prettier—white girl; a matronly woman attached to a clipped white poodle; a tired-looking woman pushing a baby carriage; a small boy being walked by a large dog.

Jason Wainwright, sitting at a window table with his back toward the bar, appeared to be fascinated at what was going on on the lower Fifth Avenue sidewalk. At any rate, he was giving his full attention to it. Now and then, he lifted a coffee cup and drank from it.

"Waiting for somebody, you think?" Tony said, his voice still low.

"Could be," Shapiro said. "Could be he did see us come in and is just waiting for a move. Could be he's just finishing his coffee."

Wainwright turned partly from the window and looked around the room, obviously for a waiter. He scribbled in the air with his right forefinger. A waiter moved toward his table.

Wainwright looked smaller at the restaurant table than

he had looked in his office at the *Sentinel.* He also looked paler, which might be because of the restaurant lighting. He looked, Shapiro thought, like a very tired old man.

The barman put glasses in front of them. The liquid in Shapiro's glass was very pale, as he had been afraid it would be. The stem of the glass was cold when he touched it.

"Suppose, Tony, we ask Mr. Wainwright to have an after-dinner drink with us? Here at the bar."

Tony Cook gave himself time for an experimental sip of his drink. Then he slipped off his stool. Wainwright was signing his dinner check when Tony reached his table. When Tony extended the invitation, Wainwright merely nodded and stood up. He walked to the bar with Tony. He sat on the stool next to Shapiro, and Tony took the one on the other side. Then Jason Wainwright spoke.

"I take it," Wainwright said, "that this is not entirely a coincidence? Your being here, I mean."

"Not entirely, Mr. Wainwright," Shapiro said. "Had you been expecting us?"

"Let's say you're not entirely unexpected," Wainwright said. "A possibility that had crossed my mind." Then he said, "No, Fred. Nothing," to the barman and, "So, gentlemen?" to Cook and Shapiro.

"A point or two," Shapiro said. "Your office door down at the paper doesn't fit tightly, Mr. Wainwright. When it's closed, your light shows under it. Did you know that, Mr. Wainwright?"

Wainwright did not answer immediately. He looked for some seconds at the mirror behind the bar.

He spoke slowly when he spoke, as if he were selecting among unfamiliar words. But all he said was, "I hadn't thought about it one way or the other, Lieutenant. But I suppose it's true of most doors. They have to have clearance to open, of course."

"Of course," Shapiro said. "But did somebody point out that light can be seen under your office door, Mr.

Wainwright? When you are in the office with the light on? At, say, a little before twelve some night? Like, say, Thursday night? Somebody like Mr. Sampson, perhaps? In Washington Square, early this afternoon?"

Wainwright looked away from the mirror then. He looked at Shapiro.

"Oughtn't you to caution me, Lieutenant?" Wainwright asked. His voice was firm. Oddly, it sounded younger to Shapiro than it had in the office the day before. "That I can remain silent if I wish? Need say nothing except in the presence of an attorney, which will be provided for me on request? Isn't that the required form, Lieutenant Shapiro?"

"In substance," Shapiro said. "The wording varies a little from state to state. You seem to know the substance, Mr. Wainwright. Yes, consider yourself cautioned, if you like. And, Tony, you'd better start taking this down."

"Am already," Tony said, and made scribbles in a notebook. On a clean page. Then he sipped from his glass.

"It's rather public here," Wainwright said. "And rather noisy, with that party going on in the next room. Aren't you going to take me in? To the station house, I suppose. Or, we could go up to my rooms. I'll want to pick up some things, if you don't mind."

"There's no great hurry," Shapiro said. "We'll finish our drinks, I think. Sure you won't have one, sir?"

"On the city?" Wainwright said. The idea seemed rather to amuse him. "All right." He raised his voice a little and said, "Fred?"

Fred was at the other end of the bar, which was apparently the service end. But he came at once.

"I've changed my mind," Wainwright told him. "The usual, I think."

Fred said, "Yes, Mr. Wainwright." But there was a hint of surprise in his voice.

"Pretty much given it up recently," Wainwright said. "Fred probably doesn't approve."

The usual turned out to be a Martell cognac, in a small brandy glass. Wainwright warmed the little glass in his hand before he drank from it.

They finished their drinks, Shapiro slowly. The sherry was dry, all right. After Fred had poured Shapiro's drink, he had put the bottle back in a glass-doored refrigerator behind the bar. Shapiro could still see the bottle. The label read "Tio Pepe." Shapiro had had experience with Tio Pepe before. He realized that many sherry drinkers regarded such experiences as pleasant. He did not. So "dry" as to be almost brittle.

They paid. They went out of the barroom through the lobby. There were chairs in the lobby and people sitting in the chairs. Most of them were elderly to aged. One was sitting in a wheelchair. An old man had crutches on the floor beside his chair. They walked by the glass doors of the main dining room, in which, now, more people were dancing. They were two tall men, one walking on each side of a shorter man with thick gray hair. They walked into a waiting elevator and the operator said, "Good evening, Mr. Wainwright."

Wainwright said, "Good evening, Charles. Stays warm, doesn't it?"

Charles agreed that it stayed warm and let them out at the eighth floor. They walked down a wide corridor, away from the Fifth Avenue side of the hotel. Wainwright used his key to open a door marked "801 A."

Wainwright's suite was of two rooms. The room they entered, the living room, had a couch and two padded chairs, one on either side of a low table. Against one wall of the rather large room was a steel table with a typewriter on it. A box of typewriter paper was on one side of the standard Underwood and, on the table's other leaf, sheets of paper with typing on them, clipped together and facedown. There was a chest of drawers on the opposite wall of the room, at the end of which ceiling-to-floor curtains were drawn.

As he opened the door, Wainwright had touched a switch and lighted two lamps, one at an end of the couch and the other on the low table between the chairs. A third lamp, tall, arching over the typewriter, did not go on. Except for the typewriter on its metal stand and an office chair in front of it, the furniture was standard hotel furniture, complete with a print of the Washington Arch on the wall over the couch. Yet the room looked lived in, as if it had adjusted itself to an occupant.

The second room, visible through an open door, was smaller. It also contained a couch, but this one had been turned down for the night.

"Sit down, gentlemen," Wainwright said, and himself sat down on the couch. "I take it you are accusing me of murder? On some evidence, I suppose? Other than the fact that light shows under my office door."

He spoke as a man might who has called a bluff. Which, Nathan Shapiro thought, in effect he has. This did not show in Nathan's long, sad face.

"Actually," Nathan Shapiro said, "we haven't accused you of anything, Mr. Wainwright. Just want to ask you a few questions. You're not under arrest."

Wainwright smiled. It was a narrow smile.

"You've cautioned me," he said. "Told me about my rights."

"At your suggestion, Mr. Wainwright. At your request, in effect."

"We're quibbling," Wainwright said. "What questions do you want to ask me?"

"Do you own a gun? A small gun? Handgun. A twenty-two or twenty-five revolver?"

"Yes. Have for years. And it's properly licensed, Lieutenant. Permit issued by your department. To a respectable citizen, who needed it for his own protection. Which you can easily verify, if you doubt my word."

"I don't doubt it," Shapiro said. "I've no doubt you have a licensed gun, Mr. Wainwright. Permits aren't too hard to come by, particularly for people like you. People of responsibility, I mean. Where is this revolver now, Mr. Wainwright?"

"In the bottom drawer of my desk at the office is where I keep it," Wainwright said. And Shapiro turned toward Cook and said, "Tony?"

"No," Tony said. "Not there now. Had a look an hour or two back. No gun in any of the desk drawers, sir."

This seemed to baffle Jason Wainwright. His pale face set in lines of bewilderment for a moment. "But—" he said, and stopped.

Puzzlement left his face. "You get forgetful when you reach my age," he said. "Incipient senility, I suppose it is. Of course the gun isn't in my desk downtown. I took it out after Claye was shot. Thought—well, that I might need it. Whoever shot poor Claye might come after others on the staff. And I was right, wasn't I? Claye and then Mr. Perryman and then Roy Sampson. A vendetta against *Sentinel* executives, it seems to be, wouldn't you say, Lieutenant?"

"Possibly," Shapiro said. "By somebody, or some group perhaps, calling itself 'The Enforcers.' Is that what you have in mind, Mr. Wainwright?"

Wainwright shook his head. He had no idea what Lieutenant Shapiro was talking about.

"All right," Shapiro said. "And is it all right if Cook uses your typewriter for a minute or two?"

Again the faint smile appeared on Wainwright's face. "And if I say no, Lieutenant?"

"I don't think you will," Shapiro said. "I don't think you really want to. Not any more."

Wainwright looked hard at Shapiro before he spoke. Then he said, "Well, well. A policeman and—and what? A psychiatrist? Should I be calling you Dr. Shapiro?"

"Just a cop, Mr. Wainwright. Trying to do a job. The typewriter?"

"I suppose you will anyway," Wainwright said. "The courts might object, I suppose. But, go ahead, Mr. Cook."

Tony went to the typewriter and fed it paper. He noted the activities of the quick brown fox. He switched on the light over the typewriter and studied under it what he had typed. He shook his head. "Hard to tell, Lieutenant," Tony Cook said. "Need a microscope, looks like. But—maybe. The *e* just a little, perhaps. Job for the lab boys."

He folded the sheet and put it in his pocket. He went back to his chair. Shapiro looked at Jason Wainwright and, rather obviously, waited for a comment. Or for a question. He got neither. After he had given Wainwright ample time to ask what the hell was going on, if he didn't know what was going on, Shapiro said, "The gun, Mr. Wainwright? And, no, we haven't got a search warrant. Or did you throw the gun away?"

"Should have, shouldn't I?" Wainwright said. "Bottom drawer of the chest in the bedroom. Under the shirts." Tony Cook went into the bedroom and opened the bottom drawer of the chest. He took a little revolver from under a neat pile of white shirts, fresh from the laundry. The gun had left a small smudge of oil under the bottom shirt.

The gun was not loaded. Tony sniffed the muzzle. It smelled of oil.

Wainwright and Nathan Shapiro watched him through the open doorway.

"Yes," Wainwright said. "I cleaned it this afternoon. Should have thrown it away, I suppose. Can't think why I—" He stopped with that. He did not look at Shapiro or at Tony Cook. He looked down, apparently at his own hands. They waited.

"Oh," Wainwright said, "perhaps I can. I suppose I wanted—well, to get it over. Because it can't really make much difference, can it?"

It was a surprising question and there was no ready answer to it Shapiro could think of. So he merely waited, and Wainwright continued to stare at his hands. Finally, he spoke.

"Comparison microscope," he said. "I suppose that's it. And is the *e* out of alignment, Mr. Cook? Like a specimen you've got? It shouldn't be. The machine is practically new. A couple of months or so. Of course, I've been using it quite a lot. Writing the history of the *Sentinel*. Would have been rather a long book. More than a hundred years to cover. A hundred and about twenty-five, actually. And fifty of them mine. Fifty-one it would have been next spring. Twenty-seven when I first went on the paper. You take shorthand, Mr. Cook?"

"Yes, sir," Tony Cook said. "Yes, Mr. Wainwright."

"Then I'll dictate you a lead," Wainwright said. "For the first edition of Monday's *Sentinel*. Not for tomorrow's *Chronicle* or *News*. Or for radio or TV. Exclusive for my newspaper. Ready?"

Cook was ready.

"Jason Wainwright, for many years editor of the New York *Sentinel*, today confessed to the fatal shooting of Roger Claye, syndicated political columnist, according to the police. The police also say that Wainwright admitted firing the shots which seriously wounded Russel Perryman, the *Sentinel*'s owner and publisher, and killed Leroy Sampson, the newspaper's managing editor."

He stopped. Then he said, "That do you, gentlemen? It's just the lead, of course. It can be marked, 'More to come,' if it's sent along in takes. Making it easy for you, aren't I? Because your evidence is a little skimpy, isn't it? Light in a crack under a door; grooves on a couple of bullets; maybe a typed *e* a shade out of alignment. Not the sort of thing a jury really likes, is it? No smoking gun, as they tried to find on Nixon. Until he handed it to them. Even the *Sentinel* had to print that, Lieutenant. Tried to bury it, but it wouldn't stay buried. Upset Perryman a good deal. Wasn't, after all, just a Democratic attempt to reverse a 'resounding victory at the polls.' Although Claye didn't really give that line up. You should have read him on it." He looked up, then, at Nathan Shapiro.

"Or," he said, "perhaps you shouldn't. You look like an honest man to me, Lieutenant. It would have gagged you. It did me. A lot of things did during the past few years. Yes, a lot of things."

"Enough to make you murder, Mr. Wainwright? Because that's what you seem to be confessing to. Hadn't you better get a lawyer?"

"So he can plead me not guilty by reason of insanity? He might get away with it, you know. An honest man probably counts as an insane man nowadays. And a man who tried to prevent a rape, of course. Obviously a crazy thing to do. I realize that; have all along, I suppose."

"A rape, Mr. Wainwright?"

"Oh, not of a woman, Lieutenant. Rape of a newspaper. Destruction of a newspaper. A newspaper—and this probably will sound insane to you, also, Lieutenant—a newspaper I've lived with for more than fifty years. Been married to, in a way. Longer than I was married to Agnes, really. We'd been married a little over forty years when she died. Six years ago, that was. Six years last month. You married, Lieutenant?"

"Yes. For quite a long time, Mr. Wainwright."

"Then maybe you can understand. It took my wife a long time to die, you see. A long and very slow time. An acutely painful time before it finally ended. I had nothing left then, you see. Nothing except the *Sentinel*. And, in a way, the paper became my second wife. Ridiculous, isn't it? But then, so many things are, aren't they? I don't suppose you can understand, can you? The feeling I got that the *Sentinel* was *my* paper. It wasn't, of course. Lester Mason's and then Perryman's. But—still, *mine*. Am I making any sense to you, Lieutenant?"

Shapiro nodded his head. He said, "Yes, Mr. Wainwright." Tony had never heard more sadness in Shapiro's almost always sad voice.

"Perryman is killing it," Wainwright said. "Killing it slowly, as my wife died slowly. Turning it into a house organ for the radical right. For the John Birchites. Do you know Claye actually put in his *Who's Who* entry that he's a member of the Birch Society? Although they keep their membership secret? And he surfaced deliberately. A strange thing to—well, boast about, wouldn't you say?"

Shapiro did not say anything.

"Young Perryman's a good kid," Wainwright said. "Been seeing a bit of him since they told me. He'll get the paper if his father dies. Run it like a newspaper, I think. Put Ed Riley in as managing editor. Riley's a good man. Knows his job. Hell of a lot better newspaperman than Sampson ever was. Make Simms editor, probably. Or take the job himself, maybe. Although he's too young for it."

"Change the policy of the paper, you mean?"

"If you mean less conservative, no, I shouldn't think so. Nor, come to that, would I. I'm as conservative, at bottom, as Russel Perryman. Well, damn near, anyway. Only—well, honest. Have the old-fashioned notion that a newspaper should print the news. All of it, whether its owner agrees with it or not. Very, as I say, old-fashioned. Almost, well, communistic to a man like Claye. He would have been the last straw, you see. Or the last dagger. Won't be now. Why I had to kill him."

"Want to tell us about that? About the killing. You don't have to, of course. Don't have to without your lawyer present. But you know that."

Wainwright merely nodded his head.

"Called me up Thursday night, Claye did. Said he thought I'd like to look at his Friday column before he sent it to the composing room. Said he thought I'd very much like to see it, since part of it concerned me. Suggested I drop by his office around midnight, after the poker game. So, well, I agreed. Only I went down a little early."

"Yes," Shapiro said. "And were in your own office with the light on when Sampson went down to look at the TV news."

"With a streak of light showing under my door," Wainwright said. "You see, I could guess pretty well what Claye was going to show me. A few things I wanted to clean up in my office, before I saw Claye. Papers, that sort of thing."

"And get your gun," Shapiro said.

"And get my gun, yes. So—it was what I knew it would be. An announcement from Perryman that, as of that day, Roger Claye would take over as editor-in-chief of the *Sentinel,* succeeding Jason Wainwright, who was retiring after long and faithful service. Made it sound as if I were a superannuated housemaid. So I read his script and shot him."

"And took his copy with you?"

"Of course. And tore it into small pieces for the nearest trash can."

"Then Perryman?"

"Yes. He'd have put somebody just as bad in my job. If he could find anybody just as bad. To run my paper even deeper into the ground."

"And Sampson?" Shapiro said. "I take it you knew his habits."

For a moment, Wainwright looked blank, his train of thought interrupted. Then his face cleared, and he nodded.

"You mean about his morning trips to the men's room, I suppose. Yes, I did. What had slipped my mind was his habit of checking up on the eleven o'clock TV news. Usually at home, of course. He's told me about it. Proving what a thorough editor he was; how he didn't miss a trick. I didn't realize that he turned the set on when he was at the office. That he would come down from the fourth floor—from the poker game—to watch the news program. Only afterward I had a more or less subconscious memory of hearing the TV going while I was waiting for Claye. He must have been playing it pretty loud. Then—well, I began to be uneasy. Began to wonder what he might have seen. Or heard. From my office. What he might have guessed. So—"

"So, on the outside chance, you took a shot at him in the

men's room. Waited for him, being pretty familiar with his habits?"

He could put it that way, Wainwright said. "And I missed. I wouldn't have tried again, I think, if he hadn't called me at The Players. Been insistent about seeing me about Thursday night. So—"

He hadn't planned on Sampson. Sampson was "a lightweight, not worth killing. Mostly just bluster." But Sampson had seen the streak of light under the door. He knew Wainwright's habits too, and got him by telephone at the bar of The Players. "Where I usually go for lunch on Saturdays." Sampson had been peremptory about seeing Wainwright and had said it was "about Thursday night."

So Wainwright had given up the idea of lunching at The Players and agreed to meet Sampson in Washington Square Park—and gone back to the hotel to get his gun, going in through the Ninth Street entrance because there was no doorman there, and going out the same way. And doing what had then seemed necessary about Leroy Sampson.

"It wasn't really," Wainwright said. "More a reflex than anything else. The animal reflex to run from danger. It was afterward that I decided not to run. Just to wait for you two to come around. Go find you, or somebody like you, if you didn't come. So—handcuffs, I suppose."

He held out his hands for the cuffs. They were frail old hands.

Cook reached for the handcuffs on his belt, but Shapiro said, "No, Tony. I think not. Not now, anyway. I'll have to talk to the captain about it, but I think Mr. Wainwright can stay here overnight. And tomorrow, probably. Arraignment Monday morning, if Weigand agrees. With a man outside his suite, of course. Although I doubt Mr. Wainwright plans to go anywhere."

The faint smile appeared again on Wainwright's lips.

"No," he said. "No place, Lieutenant. Except, of course, prison for life. Which will be six months at the outside. Perhaps as little as three, they tell me. You'd guessed that, hadn't you, Shapiro?"

Shapiro had guessed that.

"Like my wife," Wainwright said. "I hope not as long as it was with her."

* * * * *

It was after ten when Tony Cook got to Gay Street. He had had to stay with Wainwright until a man from the night shift came down to take over; he had waited until Shapiro had got in touch with Captain William Weigand and got approval. Weigand was doubtful about a preliminary charge as a material witness. He would have to consult the District Attorney's office about that.

So it was almost ten thirty when Tony Cook climbed the stairs in Gay Street. He stopped outside Rachel's door. She had said not after ten. Still. He rapped, not resolutely, on her door. There was no answer, no stirring inside.

He thought of using his key. They had exchanged keys when he had moved into the apartment above hers. He decided not to use the key; to let her sleep, in preparation for her hard day tomorrow.

He went up the stairs and into his own apartment.

He had his jacket and gun off before he looked toward his bed.

Rachel was in it. She did not appear to be asleep. She does not sleep with her eyes open.

Tony Cook finished undressing and went to bed.